MVFOL

The Missing Pieces of Me

The Missing Pieces of Me

JEAN VAN LEEUWEN

two lions

The
Missing Pieces
of Me

Text copyright © 2014 by Jean Van Leeuwen

Published by Two Lions, New York
www.apub.com

Amazon, the Amazon logo, and Two Lions
are trademarks of Amazon.com, Inc., or its affiliates.

ISBN-13: 9781477847299 (hardcover)
ISBN-10: 1477847294 (hardcover)
ISBN-13: 9781477816189 (paperback)
ISBN-10: 1477816186 (paperback)

Book design by Ryan Michaels

Library of Congress Control Number: 2014933245.

Printed in the United States of America
FIRST EDITION
10 9 8 7 6 5 4 3 2 1

To my thoughtful, insightful, wise friend, Judy

Broken

Momma says I'm a bad girl.

That's what Momma says. I ask her why and she says, "You know why."

Like yesterday with the teapot. The one that used to be Gramma Emmeline's. She made her tea in it every day of her grown-up life, Momma says.

I'd an idea to surprise her when she got home from work. She'd be saying how her feet hurt and her back was aching bad, and I'd have her slippers set out by her chair and her tea made in Gramma Emmeline's teapot. And I'd make sure the trailer was picked up and Ruth Ann wasn't whining like usual and Jackson wasn't playing trucks where she'd trip the minute she walked in.

So I washed all the dishes in the sink and made Ruth Ann pick up her scattered-around toys.

"Why do I have to?" Right off Ruth Ann started to whine.

"For Momma," I told her.

Her bottom lip was still poked out.

"To make her happy," I said.

Ruth Ann brightened up. "Maybe she'll bring us Tootsie Pops."

She helped some and then I got her coloring at the counter and Jackson watching cartoons. I fixed the pillows in Momma's chair and set her slippers by it, waiting. Next came the tea water. I put on the kettle and got out the tea bags and Momma's cup with the purple butterfly.

Everything was ready. I climbed up on the counter, careful as could be, and took down Gramma Emmeline's teapot, all fancy with its pink roses and gold rim. I held it tight to make sure I didn't drop it. And then my foot stepped on one of Ruth Ann's crayons. And I slipped.

Gramma Emmeline's teapot crashed to the floor.

"Oh!" was all I could say. I was that surprised.

"It's broken," said Ruth Ann. "You broke Momma's teapot."

Jackson scooted over on his backside.

"Boke," he said, picking up one of the pieces.

"Don't touch it!" I jumped down and took it before he could cut himself.

Jackson started bawling.

"Momma's gonna be mad," chirped Ruth Ann in her singsong voice.

And the teakettle was whistling so loud, it could curl your ears.

That's when Momma opened the door.

She saw the teapot first thing, dropped her grocery bag, and went down on her knees on the linoleum floor. Holding up the piece with the biggest flower, she looked about to cry.

"What happened?" she asked.

It was her quiet voice, the one that came just before she started yelling.

"Weezie did it!" Ruth Ann said right away.

"I was going to surprise you, Momma," I said real fast, turning off the screeching kettle. "See? I got your slippers and pillows for your back and I was making your tea, special in Gramma Emmeline's teapot. I'm sorry, Momma."

Her eyes got narrow and her eyebrows came down. Like a dark cloud before a rainstorm.

"That was my momma's teapot! About the only thing I had left of hers after she died. Did I say you could touch it, you clumsy girl? Why do you think I kept it up there?"

The cloud had broken.

"Maybe it's not ruined," I said. "Maybe we can glue it back together."

I was talking too much. That could make her madder. But sometimes if I kept talking, she calmed down. I kneeled down and gathered up the pieces.

"See, Momma? The top isn't even broken."

"Give them to me."

She held out her hands and, carefully, I put the pieces in them. Momma walked over to the garbage can, popped the lid, and dropped them in.

"What's broken can't be fixed," she said.

She plunked down in her chair with her eyes closed. Likely she was getting one of her bad headaches, and it was my fault.

"Should I get you one of your pills?" I asked.

Momma shook her head.

"I'm sorry," I said again. "Don't be mad, Momma."

I picked up the bag to put away the groceries. But

4

before I could take out the Wonder Bread, Momma opened her eyes.

They were hard and mean.

"Get out of my sight!" she barked. "I can't stand to look at you."

I felt like I was shrinking, folding inside myself till I was smaller than Jackson, smaller than Ruth Ann's Barbie doll.

"Yes, Momma."

I walked back to the little bedroom I shared with my sister and brother and climbed up on the top bunk. I didn't feel like doing my homework or reading my library book about dolphins. I didn't feel like doing anything. I just lay there.

How could I have broken Gramma Emmeline's teapot? I should have looked before I stepped. I was clumsy like Momma said. I couldn't do things right.

Staring at the faded yellow-dot curtains Gramma Emmeline had made, I listened to the TV and Ruth Ann whining about why couldn't she have a Tootsie Pop. And I waited.

But Momma never did call me for supper.

Gramma Emmeline

"I'm sorry about your teapot," I whispered to the curtains.

Was Gramma Emmeline in the curtains? Or in her broken teapot? Where did you go after you died? Were any little pieces of you left behind?

I thought I remembered Gramma Emmeline sewing those curtains on her machine that made that nice whirring sound when she pushed down the pedal. I used to like to sit on the floor and watch her make it go. That was when I was about four, like Ruth Ann is now. She took care of me while Momma was at work.

Gramma Emmeline was sick even then.

"I love my sugar," she'd say to me, "but that doctor won't let me have none. On account of the diabetes, you know."

I didn't know what she was talking about, of course. All I knew was Gramma Emmeline had a big, warm lap and she called me by my real name, Grace Louise, and did my hair with flower barrettes and made gooey peanut butter sandwiches for lunch. And after lunch, we each got to pick a chocolate from the box she kept hidden in her kitchen drawer.

"Just one now, Grace Louise," she'd tell me. "On account of the sugar."

But most days we had two.

"Don't tell anyone," she'd say, laughing. Gramma Emmeline had a laugh that rippled through her body so if you were sitting on her lap, it was all bouncy. I remembered that.

And also the Easter rabbit she gave me one time. Pink with a straw hat that got smooshed right away and a ruffly dress she sewed on her machine. What happened to that rabbit anyway?

Soon after the rabbit, everything changed. Momma got married to Tommy with the blond hair and Ruth Ann came, crying all the time, and we moved to the trailer. And Gramma Emmeline only came to see us sometimes.

"My legs hurt too much," she said. They swelled up so, they looked like elephant legs to me. Her face was puffy too. It was like she was getting blown up like a balloon.

Then one day I came home from first grade and skinny-as-a-stick Mrs. Holcomb from next door was there instead of Momma. She said Momma had to go to the hospital because my gramma had a heart attack.

Mrs. Holcomb was there for hours. She didn't know about babies and couldn't get Ruth Ann to stop crying, so I had to give her bread and sugar. Mrs. Holcomb kept telling me to go to bed, but I wouldn't so we watched TV until finally Momma and Tommy came back. He was holding her up like she'd forgotten how to walk and she was crying so hard, she couldn't talk.

"Your gramma's gone," Tommy told me.

Gone? What did that mean?

But just like that, she was. Gone. I never saw Gramma Emmeline ever again. How could she be here one day and then gone forever?

Momma didn't talk for the longest time. She cried and cried, sitting in her chair holding the tissue box. Her eyes got so swollen, they were just little slits at the top of her face.

Mrs. Holcomb stayed with Ruth Ann and me for the funeral and after that, real slowly, Momma got to be herself again. She and Tommy took me to see where Gramma Emmeline was buried under the grass and we put daffodils by her gravestone.

I couldn't stop thinking about why my nice gramma had to die.

"What's a heart attack?" I asked Momma.

She said she didn't rightly know but she thought Gramma Emmeline's heart just got tired and gave out.

"Was it on account of the sugar?" I asked.

"Maybe."

I felt a jolt someplace in my insides. Gramma Emmeline ate all those chocolates while she was taking care of me. Was it my fault her heart gave out?

I didn't tell Momma that, though. She had enough troubles with Tommy up and deciding one day to go be a soldier. I heard them arguing about it every night through the thin walls of the trailer. But he was bound he'd go, and a few weeks later off he went to training camp, waving at us with the biggest smile I'd ever seen on his face.

It was only four months after that she got the news. Tommy fell off a truck and got run over. Gone, just like Gramma Emmeline.

It took a long time for Momma to stop crying after Tommy. Mrs. Holcomb was with us all the time, and Momma lost her job at Porky's Ribs, and for a while it looked like she'd never leave the trailer. Finally she did, and she got the job she has now at Pancake Heaven. Only she never got happy again.

Instead of thinking about that, which made my stomach hurt, I thought about Gramma Emmeline.

I wished I could remember her face. Little bits I could see, like her hair frizzed up and colored orange like a carrot. Her elephant legs. And the big flower apron she wore when she was cooking. But not her face.

Closing my eyes, I thought about nothing. And then, when I was just about to slip into sleep, I saw her.

She was smiling at me. Her face was round, not puffy round like at the end, but the way it was when she took care of me. Her cheeks had those two spots of color she put on to match her dark lipstick. Her eyes were watery blue. Blue like sky. Watery because even though she needed them, she didn't like to wear the glasses that hung on a chain around her neck.

Gramma Emmeline was smiling such a loving smile at me. I wasn't sure if I was awake or asleep, but I saw her sitting underneath the big pecan tree out back of her house. I sat across from her, and next to me, on another chair, was my rabbit. Patty Sue, I called her. I remembered now.

A little table sat between us. In the middle was a box of chocolates. And next to it, steaming hot, was her teapot with the roses.

"Will you have a cup of tea, Grace Louise?" she asked. "And how about you, Patty Sue?"

It wasn't really tea, just Ovaltine.

"Yes, please," I said. "And a chocolate too."

"Only one," she said, laughing.

And I knew she didn't care about the teapot being broken, and anyway it wasn't broken now.

"Thank you, Gramma," I said.

A Traveling Man

Of course the teapot wasn't fixed. That was just a dream or some kind of craziness inside my head. I knew it in the morning when I looked in the garbage can. There were the pieces, still broken.

"Wishing don't make it so," Gramma Emmeline used to say.

While Momma was at work, I tried to fix the teapot. I found some of the pieces and tried to put them together, but I couldn't get the roses to match. As hard as I tried, I couldn't make them fit. Finally, I had to give up. I couldn't bear to just throw away Gramma Emmeline's teapot, though. So I put the little pieces in one of Jackson's socks and stuck it behind my underwear in the little chest I shared with Ruth Ann.

The teapot really was ruined. And Gramma Emmeline was still dead, too. I wished hard that she wasn't. If she was here, I could ask her the question Momma won't answer no matter how many times I ask her. Two questions, really.

Who is my daddy? And where is he at now?

Gramma Emmeline would answer, I bet. But Momma just shakes her head and all of a sudden has to go change Jackson's diaper. Or her face turns hard like one of those clay faces we made in kindergarten and she says, "Better you don't know." Then if I say, "But I want to know," that dark cloud comes down and she starts yelling.

Everybody has a daddy. I know that. Ruth Ann's is Tommy, who everyone thinks was a hero even though he was killed in training camp. His picture in his army uniform sits next to Momma's bed, and Ruth Ann is always looking at it and saying, "My daddy was a soldier." And Jackson's is Roy who comes to see him on his motorcycle but never brings any money, so Momma gets mad and sends him away.

"Come back when you can feed your son!" she yells at him.

I've been thinking about my daddy a lot lately on account of Ruby Hill. She's in my class at school. She's scrawny as a chicken and has a pointy little nose she likes to stick into everybody's business. On the bus she'll up and ask any rude question she can think of, in a loud voice so the whole bus can hear.

One day last week she sat down next to me.

"So, Weezie," she said out of the blue. "How come you have no daddy?"

Loud, of course. The boys behind me stopped talking. I felt like I had to say something.

"I do so have one," I said.

"Well, I never see him around town," said Ruby.

I didn't know what to answer. Then I remembered something I'd heard Gramma Emmeline say one time. I wasn't sure if it was about my daddy or someone else.

"That's because he's a traveling man," I said.

"Really?" A smirky little smile crept across her face. I could tell she had lots more questions she was dying to ask. "Where's he travel to?"

"Uh, everywhere. The whole country."

We were passing the diner where the truck stop

14

was, and I saw the big rigs parked outside. That gave me an idea.

"He drives a truck. Way bigger than that silver one."

One of the boys whistled. That kind of got me going.

"Not just here in Oklahoma," I went on. My voice didn't sound like me. It was bright and shiny. "He's been out to California and New York City and even Mexico."

I couldn't seem to stop myself. "You know what he brought me from there? A real sombrero."

Farley Wilcox tapped me on the shoulder. "Can I see it sometime?"

This was getting bad. I wasn't used to telling lies. I couldn't think fast enough.

"Um—I don't have it anymore. My baby brother chewed it up."

Ruby was staring at me with her pale blue eyes. She reminded me of our last year's teacher, Mrs. Mudd. No matter what you told her, she always looked like she didn't believe you.

"So that's why your daddy's never home? 'Cause he's driving that big truck all over the place?"

"Oh, he comes home sometimes," I said. "And brings us presents and lots of money."

Now why did I say that?

"Then how come you live in that trailer park?" Ruby snapped back.

"We like it there," I said just as fast.

That sounded lame even to me. Ruby grinned, like she'd just won something.

"Well," she said, "my daddy's always home and he brings us soda pop from the 7-Eleven and plays with us after supper every night."

That would be her and her five brothers. I knew who her daddy was, and he was no great shakes. He worked under cars at Roy Crowley's garage and wore greasy overalls and looked like he never saw the light of day.

But like Ruby said, he was always home.

From out of nowhere, I felt tears starting at the back of my eyes. I looked out the window so she wouldn't see.

"Well," I said, "next time my daddy's home, he's going to take me on a trip, just him and me in his truck. All the way to Florida. To Disney World."

Oh, I had her now. She wasn't grinning anymore. The boys behind us were saying, "Hey, cool! Can we come too?"

"And you know what else?" I said, calm as could

be. Seemed like I was starting to get the hang of this lying thing.

"What?" said Farley.

I waited to make sure they were all listening. Just about everyone on the bus now.

"My daddy and me, we're going to swim with the dolphins."

The Investigation

Momma had the late shift on Saturdays, so I didn't have to watch Ruth Ann and Jackson. I had practically the whole day free. And I knew what I wanted to do.

First thing was to pay a visit to Mrs. Holcomb in the next trailer.

Hers was the nicest in the whole park. White with green shutters and pretty flower pots by the front door. I knocked.

Right off, her dog started yapping. That made me smile. It thinks it's a killer dog when it's just a little puffball. Muffin is its name.

"Muffy, hush up! That's my good girl."

Mrs. Holcomb came to the door carrying her dog. "Weezie! Come in."

As soon as I got inside, that silly dog turned into a love machine, wagging its tail so hard it about knocked itself over.

"Sit down, Weezie," said Mrs. Holcomb. "Is your momma alright? Is Jackson sick again?"

I sat down on her flowered love seat. Mrs. Holcomb's trailer was as nice inside as outside, all done up with curtains that matched the love seat, and the TV in a real wooden cabinet.

"He's fine, and so is Momma. I just wanted to ask you something."

Mrs. Holcomb looked relieved. She had kindly eyes. That's one thing I always noticed about her.

"If you need me, I'm here to help. Now what did you want to ask me?"

I hadn't thought about how to ask the question. Muffin was licking my hand now, her soft tongue cleaning each finger.

"It's just, I was wondering. Did you know my daddy?"

"Oh no, honey, I didn't. You know I just moved here a few years back, after Mr. Holcomb passed on."

I remembered that now. Of course she didn't know him.

"Well, I'm sorry to bother you," I said.

"It's no bother. Won't you stay and have a soda pop?"

"Thank you, but I can't. I have to go someplace."

She walked me to the door. "You don't remember your daddy at all, honey?" she asked.

"No, ma'am."

"Well, that's a shame. But Weezie, you're such a nice girl. I'll bet he was a nice man, too."

I walked away, her words bouncing off the walls inside my head. Mrs. Holcomb thought I was a nice girl. That made me feel good. But then I remembered she didn't know I was clumsy and broke things and told lies. Mrs. Holcomb didn't know me at all.

I hadn't told her a single lie, though. Not today.

"Hey, Weezie!"

It was my friend Calvin on his red bike with the fat tires.

"I was just coming to look for you," I said.

"What for?"

"I thought we could ride to town. I'm doing an investigation."

Calvin's round face looked confused. Even though he was a year younger, he was bigger than me. Calvin was big all over. Only a little slow in his thinking. Some kids made fun of him, but speaking of nice, he was the nicest person I knew. He never told lies and he'd do anything anyone asked. He liked to go to town, on account of the cars. Calvin loved cars more than anything. He always had a few little Matchbox ones in his pockets.

"What are we investing?" he asked.

"Investigating. My daddy. I'm trying to find out about him."

Most people, like Ruby, would ask all kinds of questions. But Calvin just said, "Hop on."

We rode to town, me behind him, my arms wrapped around the gray sweatshirt he always wore. On the way, I tried to think who I could ask about my daddy.

Momma's friend Marcella seemed like the best place to start. She colored hair at Dora Lee's House of Beauty. Momma's dream, she'd told me once, was for her and Marcella to open their own beauty shop. They'd even given it a name: "Heavenly Hair." But they both had too little money and too many kids to do it. Momma looked sad when she said that.

Calvin was about to stop at Dora Lee's when I saw Momma's little pea-green car parked out front.

"Not here!" I said, poking him in the back.

"What's wrong?"

"I can't go in there. Momma's inside."

Sometimes, if Marcella isn't too busy, Momma takes Ruth Ann to get her blond hair curled and her face made up. She comes home looking like a painted doll, but Momma says she's her little princess. She talks about entering her in some beauty pageant when she's a little older.

"Where do you want to go then?"

I didn't know, but I was glad now I hadn't talked to Marcella. She'd likely tell Momma and Momma would just get mad.

Then I thought of Uncle Billy Bruner. He wasn't anyone's uncle I knew of, people just called him that. He lived next door to Gramma Emmeline. They used to sit on Gramma's porch drinking ice tea, and he'd fix things in her house that got broken. I remember he gave me piggyback rides a few times when she took care of me.

"Keep going," I told Calvin, "and turn on Church Street."

As we passed Dora Lee's, I couldn't help peering in. Sure enough, there was Ruth Ann sitting up in Marcella's chair. She wasn't whining now, I bet.

Then we were on Gramma Emmeline's old street with the Eternal Life Church on the corner. Her house was number sixteen. It looked like it used to except the porch was painted yellow now. I kind of wished I could go inside and see if it was still the same, but I kind of didn't in case it wasn't. Which it probably wouldn't be.

I tapped Calvin on the shoulder. "Here."

Uncle Billy's house looked like I remembered it, but rundown. He hadn't been fixing things that were broken, like the front steps.

"Do you want to come in with me?" I asked.

"Nah, I'll wait."

Calvin wasn't much for talking to grownups. He'd rather sit on the curb and watch the cars go by.

"Okay. See ya later, Alligator."

Calvin laughed. He liked that joke.

I climbed the broken steps and rang the doorbell.

"Yes?"

A woman I didn't know opened the door. She had on a sweatshirt with a smiley face, but her face wasn't smiling.

"Uh," I said. "Does Uncle Billy Bruner still live here?"

She looked me up and down, like maybe I was a criminal come to steal Uncle Billy's money.

"My gramma used to live next door. Emmeline Dawson. She was a friend of Uncle Billy's. I just stopped by to see how he's doing."

Well, that was another lie. I hadn't thought of Uncle Billy till a few minutes ago.

"Pa ain't doing so good," the woman said.

"Could I see him? Just for a few minutes?"

"S'pose so."

I followed her into a dark room. At first I didn't see anyone, but then a quavery voice said, "Who was that at the door, Shirley?" I saw someone huddled under a blanket in a recliner chair.

"Little girl wants to see you," said Shirley.

"It's me, Uncle Billy," I said. "Grace Louise, Emmeline Dawson's grandbaby. You used to ride me piggyback a long time ago."

Uncle Billy had been a hearty-looking man. Now he'd shrunk down to barely a bump under the blanket. He peered at me with watery eyes.

"Can't say I recall that."

It looked like I'd come here for nothing, just like with Mrs. Holcomb.

"Give me a minute," he said. "I don't see so good and Shirley thinks my brain is addled too. Seems like Emmeline had a grandbaby she cared for."

"That's me, Uncle Billy," I said.

"Well, I wouldn't have known you. Guess you've changed some."

"I'm going on eleven this summer."

A smile flitted across his thin face. "Your gramma and me had some good times sitting on her porch. That woman sure loved to laugh. Where are you at now?"

"We're out at Happy Days Trailer Park," I said. "Me and Momma and my little sister and brother. Momma's working at Pancake Heaven."

"That sounds real nice."

"Uncle Billy," I said. "I was wondering. Do you remember my daddy?"

"Let me think." He rubbed his chin whiskers. "No, I can't recall knowing him. Heard about him some, though."

I caught my breath. "What did you hear?"

"He come from out of town, I believe. And your gramma wasn't real fond of him. He run out on your momma or some such thing."

I pretty much knew that.

"Do you remember his name?"

"You got me there. Could've been one of them cowboy names. Randy or Wayne or one of them."

That was something. Not what I'd been hoping for, but something.

Shirley spoke up all of a sudden. "You've had your visit. It's time for Pa's lunch."

"It was good to see you, Uncle Billy," I said. "Oh,

one more thing. Do you know if my daddy drove a truck?"

Uncle Billy's eyes were closed, like he'd fallen asleep. But then he opened them and said, "Matter of fact, he did. Had a little old pickup. Your gramma used to say he was fonder of it than anything human. She was kind of mad about that."

Shirley had me by the elbow now, steering me to the door.

"You've tired him out," she said. "I told you he was doing poorly."

"I'm sorry," I said. "Bye, Uncle Billy. And thank you!"

I climbed back on Calvin's bike and we started for home. As we passed Gramma Emmeline's house, I looked up at her porch again. Suddenly I remembered something.

I'm three or four, sitting on Gramma Emmeline's cozy lap on that porch, waiting for Momma to come home from work. While we wait, we sing songs. My favorite is "Row, Row, Row Your Boat," because every time we get to the end, we change it to something silly.

"Life is but a banana!" I sing, and Gramma's deep-down laugh bounces me up and down.

"Life is but a peanut butter sandwich!" Gramma sings, and I laugh so hard I almost wet my pants.

Then I see Momma coming up the steps. I quick jump down from Gramma's lap and run to meet her.

She catches me in her arms and lifts me up high.

"And whose little girl are you?" she asks.

"Yours," I say.

She gives me the biggest, brightest smile.

Swimming
with the Dolphins

When I got home, sure enough Ruth Ann was made up like a princess. Her hair was curled and her cheeks had bright spots of color. Marcella had even pasted on fake eyelashes, which looked sort of funny and made Ruth Ann blink. She was wearing purple nail polish. She looked happy as a bee buzzing in clover, as Gramma Emmeline used to say.

"Aren't I pretty?" she said. "Marcella says if I'm not Miss Oklahoma when I grow up, she'll be a monkey's uncle. What's a monkey's uncle?"

"A monkey, I guess," I said. She did look pretty in spite of the blinking.

"Can I try on my new dress now, Momma?" she asked.

Ruth Ann's gramma in Florida was always sending her dresses when it wasn't even her birthday or Christmas either.

"Not now," said Momma. "Can't you see I'm making supper?"

She was frying up hotdogs, already wearing her pink Pancake Heaven uniform with the cloud patch that said, "Hi, I'm Charlene." I could tell right away she was in one of her moods.

"Please, Momma?"

Ruth Ann was starting to whine. That was never good, specially when Momma was in a mood and getting ready to go to work.

"Please, please, PLEASE?" Each time she said it, Ruth Ann's voice got higher.

Momma flipped the hotdogs so fast, grease splashed all over the stove.

"I said not now!"

"Later," I told Ruth Ann. "After supper we'll play Beauty Pageant and you can twirl your skirt."

"No, now! I want to twirl now!"

"Wirl!" piped up Jackson.

I forgot that was his favorite thing to do. Next

thing, the two of them were whirling in circles, laughing like crazy. But then Jackson bumped into the TV and fell on his bottom and Ruth Ann smacked her elbow and they both started bawling.

Momma spun around from the stove. "Now see what you did!"

"Me?" It was Ruth Ann started it with her whining.

"You said 'twirl.' You know that gets Jackson going! Don't you have any sense? I'm trying to make supper and get to work on time so Frankie doesn't fire me. And where were you all day? Can't you stay around and help?"

All of a sudden, black smoke billowed up from the stove.

"Now see what you made me do!" Momma yelled. "Your supper's all burnt. Well, you'll just have to make something else. I have to go to work."

She grabbed her purse and banged out the door.

Tears stung my eyes. Momma was so unfair. I wanted to run out the door and keep running until I found Gramma Emmeline still alive at her house and bury my head in her lap. I wanted to be small as Jackson so someone would take care of me.

He was still crying, his nose a mess of snot.

"Boo-boo," he said.

I picked him up and kissed his boo-boos. I had

to kiss Ruth Ann's elbow too, and then she asked, "What are we having for supper?"

"P and J," I said, which was her favorite, so she didn't whine but helped me spread peanut butter on slices of Wonder Bread.

Jackson was worn out and climbed into his crib right after supper. And Ruth Ann didn't make a fuss when her fake eyelashes fell off. She twirled a little in her new dress and then she went to bed too.

It was quiet for once. I flicked the channels on the TV, but none of my favorite nature programs were on. I liked to watch baby animals taking their first walk. Or amazing-colored birds flitting around the jungle. Or goats climbing mountains so steep, you just knew they'd fall off, but they didn't. I liked seeing far-off places so different from our dusty town. I'd never get to really see them, but I wished I could.

Then a commercial came on. A cowboy-looking man was driving a pickup loaded with hay. He had hay-colored hair and smiling eyes and big, strong hands on the wheel. Which made me think of my daddy. He'd had a pickup, Uncle Billy said.

What if this man was my daddy? He could be. My daddy might have driven his pickup out to Hollywood and some movie person saw him and said you're so handsome, we're going to put you in the movies. And by the way, would you like to do a truck commercial?

Well, maybe not. My daddy likely didn't have hay-colored hair because then I'd have it too, like Ruth Ann had Tommy-colored hair. Too bad.

No, that wasn't my daddy. But inside my head, I started spinning out a picture. Of my daddy and me in his truck. Not some little old pickup, but one of those big rigs at the truck stop like I'd told Ruby about when I made up that story about my daddy. It could be true. Hadn't Gramma Emmeline said he was a traveling man?

So there we are, my daddy and me, roaring down the highway. And it's black outside except for our headlights poking holes in the night, picking up houses and gas stations and palm trees at the side of the road. Yes, palm trees because we're in Florida now, heading for where they let you swim with the dolphins. We'd swim together, just him and me, with those dolphins, friendly as could be, swimming all around us.

Inside the truck, the radio is playing country music, and my daddy and I are singing along. And we're laughing because the song is about a broken heart, but our hearts aren't broken. We're happy.

I look over at my daddy and see his dirt-brown hair

*like mine and his eyes filled with laughing. He looks back
and says, "I'm real glad you found me, Grace Louise."*

It came over me then that this could happen for
real. I knew my daddy loved trucks, and Gramma
Emmeline said he was a traveling man. I was sure
now she'd said it about my daddy. So I bet he was
driving one of those big rigs right now.

All I had to do was find him.

Old Horse Face

Wouldn't you know it. Monday morning on the bus Ruby started in again with her nosy questions.

"So, Weezie," she said, real friendly. "When are you and your daddy going on that trip to Disney World?"

"Uh—" I didn't know what to say. You had to be a fast thinker when Ruby was on your case, and I was barely awake.

She didn't give me a minute, just pounced like that yellow cat that's always hanging around our trailer looking for mice.

"Or was that just a story? I bet you're not really going."

"I am," I said. "I'm just not sure when. Probably after school is out."

That was good. I wouldn't be seeing her then.

"You said you were going the next time your daddy comes home. He's not coming home till summer?"

Why'd she have to remember that? I had to think fast.

"Sure he is. Probably for Easter. He's going to bring me the biggest chocolate rabbit you ever saw. But we can't go then."

"Why not?"

Why did she have to ask all these questions?

"Because it's a holiday. You have to be home on a holiday."

Ruby had that little smile again that made me want to smash something into her face.

"Then you should bring him to our Easter egg hunt at Calvary Baptist. We give out good prizes, like a giant jar of jelly beans and a free car wash. He'd like that, driving a truck and all. And there's a pancake breakfast too."

I knew what she was up to. I was wide-awake now.

"That would be nice," I said. "Only he might not want to go anyplace. He'll be all tired out from driving."

I was tired out from thinking up these lies, and

we hadn't even gotten to school yet. What would she come back with now?

She gave me a look that said she was working on it. But just then the bus slowed down and turned in at Clyde B. Page Elementary School.

Just in time, I thought.

I got up quick, but she was right behind me, whispering in my ear.

"Bet you're not really going to Disney World."

Something inside me went crazy then. As I stepped off the bottom step, I stuck out my foot and tripped Ruby. She fell down in a heap.

"Hey, whatcha do that for?"

Jumping up, she stuck her nose in my face.

That made me madder. I pushed her down again, but she popped right up, swinging her fists like one of those boxing guys on TV.

Uh-oh. She was a scrawny little thing, but those big brothers of hers must have taught her about fighting. I'd never hit anyone in my life so I stepped back from her flying fists and pushed her down and sat on her. Just to keep her from hitting me.

"Girls!"

Mrs. Pinto, the bus driver, was staring down at us, along with all the bus kids. Calvin's mouth was wide open like he couldn't believe what he was seeing.

I couldn't believe it either, specially when Mrs. Pinto grabbed Ruby and me by the elbows and dragged us to the principal's office.

"She started it!" Ruby was squealing, and Calvin was saying, "You shouldn't-a-done that, Weezie."

I knew it. I was in big trouble now.

Mrs. Pinto sat us down outside the principal's office and told Calvin to go to his class. He didn't want to, but he went.

"Mr. McCracken will see you in a few minutes," she told us. Then she was gone and it was just me and Ruby sitting in the hall, waiting.

What was going to happen? I'd heard the boys talking about Mr. McCracken. They called him "Old Horse Face" and said he was mean. What kind of punishment would we get? Or would it just be me that got punished because I started it? I'd never been to the principal's office before.

Ruby swung her feet. She rubbed her knee where it poked out of a hole in her jeans.

Good. I hoped it was real sore. Maybe now she'd leave me alone.

But no, she kept smirking at me, like she knew something I didn't know.

Then she said it. "He's gonna call your momma."

Oh, that was the worst thing that could happen!

Momma would come to school and find out all the lies I'd told about my daddy. And now this trouble too.

Would Mr. McCracken really call her? Ruby should know. I bet she'd sat in this chair before.

I didn't answer, but she knew she'd got me. She sat there smiling her nasty little smile.

The secretary took her in first. I listened to see if she got yelled at, but I couldn't hear anything. Likely she was telling Mr. McCracken she didn't do a thing, that I just tripped her for no reason and I should get kicked out of school.

That would be a bad punishment. I liked school.

It seemed like hours before Ruby came out, and when she did she walked by me without saying a word. Then it was my turn.

Mr. McCracken was sitting behind a big desk covered with papers. He did look kind of like a horse, I thought, with his long face and big nose and combed-back gray hair.

"Sit down, Grace Louise," he said. No smile or anything.

I sat facing his desk. I could hardly see him behind the stacks of papers, but I felt him staring at me. He didn't say anything else. The clock on the wall buzzed. It said 9:07. On the windowsill was a plant with yellow leaves.

Should I say something, like, "I'm sorry"? That might be good. But I was afraid if I opened my mouth, nothing would come out.

Maybe he was going to keep up his mean stare till I started to cry. That could be his plan. I squeezed my eyes shut. *Don't cry,* I told them, and opened them again.

Mr. McCracken was still staring at me. "Why don't you tell me what happened," he said.

What could I say? If I told him the whole story, he'd know about my lies and he'd be sure to tell Momma. But I didn't want to make up new lies. It was getting hard to remember them all.

"Uh, well—" I started. "Ruby was teasing me on the bus and I got mad. And I—um—tripped her and then we got into a fight. And she kept hitting me so I sat on her to make her stop. That's all. And I'm sorry."

There. I'd told the truth even though I'd left out a few details.

"I see."

Mr. McCracken folded his hands, tapping the fingers up and down. He was thinking up my punishment, I could tell. I bet he was going to call Momma. Inside my head, I could see her sitting in the chair I was sitting in now.

Ruby's there too, and it's like a trial on TV. In her phony, good-girl voice she tells Momma all the bad things I did. "She said her daddy was taking her to Disney World. She said they were going to swim with the dolphins. She said he drives a big truck all over the place and he brought her a sombrero from Mexico. And when I told her she was lying, she beat me up."

Mr. McCracken shakes his head. "She has to be punished," he says.

Momma looks at me with her disappointed eyes.

"I knew she was bad," she says, "but this is even worse than I thought. She deserves the worst punishment you can think up."

I couldn't stand it.

"Please don't call my momma," I begged. "And don't kick me out of school. I won't do it again, I promise."

Mr. McCracken looked surprised. He tapped his fingers some more. Then he smiled. He actually smiled at me.

"Well, Grace Louise," he said. "Being sorry is the most important thing. You can go on to your class now."

"Really?" I couldn't believe I wasn't getting any punishment.

"Just remember what you said. You won't do it again."

"Yes, sir."

I left his office practically flying. Mr. McCracken wasn't mean. He wasn't giving me any punishment. And best of all, he wasn't going to call Momma! She wouldn't find out about my lies.

For sure I'd keep my promise. I'd stay away from Ruby. If she sat down next to me, I'd move. If she talked to me, I wouldn't answer. That way I'd never get in trouble.

And I'd never tell another lie.

Mac and Cheese

Not only was I going to stop telling lies, I decided. From now on, I was going to work hard at being good. I'd show Momma she was wrong about me.

I started right in. I thought of all the things Momma didn't like and wrote them down. Like rules for myself.

1. *No getting on Momma's nerves.*
2. *No talking back.*
3. *No breaking things.*
4. *No asking questions. Specially about my daddy.*
5. *No arguing.*
6. *No saying twirl in front of Jackson.*
7. *No telling lies. Very important!*

Those were all the noes I could think of. On the other side of the paper I made a list of good things I should do.

1. Pick up the trailer.
2. Help Momma. Specially on Saturdays.
3. Do what she says.
4. Keep Ruth Ann and Jackson from bothering her when she's tired out from her job.
5. Fix supper sometimes so she doesn't have to do it.

That was all I could think of for yeses. I had more noes than yeses, but I could always add on.

I read over my rules a few times so I wouldn't forget them. And the next afternoon after school, I started being the new, good me.

First, I washed the gummy breakfast dishes. Then I put away Ruth Ann's and Jackson's toys. And then I looked on the shelf for something to fix for supper.

Macaroni and cheese—that might be it. I read the directions on the box. All you had to do was cook the noodles, add milk and the cheese packet, and stir. Easy. Momma would be so happy when she got home and saw supper all ready. I went outside to wait for Ruth Ann and Jackson to get home from daycare.

It was a warm, spring-like day. I saw Mrs. Holcomb had new flowers in her pots. Pansies. If only I could pick some for Momma. But that would be stealing. In the weeds, I saw another flower. It was only a dandelion, but they were pretty too. I could put some in a glass on the counter.

I began picking, and the next minute I heard a car. It was Mrs. Atchley dropping off Ruth Ann and Jackson. She and her little boy Bobby lived four trailers down.

"I want some!" cried Ruth Ann the minute she saw my flowers.

I waved to Mrs. Atchley, and we all starting looking for dandelions.

Jackson reached for one and fell down. He started to cry.

"Look, Jackson," I said and gave him one of mine. What did he do but put it in his mouth.

"Don't do that! The pretty flower is for Momma."

Jackson was really bawling now. Then I heard something louder. A motorcycle coming up the hill.

Not Roy, I thought. *Not now.*

But it was. Jackson's daddy come to see him even though Momma told him not to. And just when I was trying to make things nice for her.

"Hi, Weezie," he said. "How's my boy?"

"You can't come here," I said right off. "You know what Momma says."

"Aw, come on." He gave me one of his slow, sideways grins and took off his helmet, shaking back his long, black hair. "I just want to see how he's doing."

I knew what he was up to, coming when Momma wasn't home, trying to sweet-talk me into a visit with Jackson. Well, it wasn't going to work. I could be as tough as Momma.

"He's fine," I said, real short like she would. "You can go now."

"Now Weezie," he said. "You know it's not right for me not to see my own son. It's not natural."

I had to admit he had something there. And I liked Roy. He'd always been nice to me. But Momma didn't.

"Did you bring money?" I asked.

Roy looked down at the dirt. "You know I lost my job at the Mobil station. But I was at the 7-Eleven today. If I get that job, I'll bring money next time. Just let me hold my boy. Please?"

I didn't know what to say. It only seemed right to me, but Momma would think different.

"Three minutes," I said. "Then you have to go."

Roy shot me another grin and picked up Jackson.

"Hey, little buddy, remember me? I'm your daddy."

45

Jackson was full of grins himself, specially when Roy put him on his bike.

"Vroom!" said Roy.

"Room!" said Jackson.

They looked so happy together, it gave me a funny feeling. Glad for Jackson and Roy. Sad for me with no daddy. And a little scared. What if Roy rode off with him?

"That's your three minutes," I told him. "You better go. Momma's coming home early today."

She wasn't. I just told him that to scare him. Oops, I'd gone and told another lie.

It worked. Roy said, "So long, buddy. And thanks, Weezie. Next week I'll bring him a present, just wait and see."

He rode off. Of course, Jackson started bawling again. And Ruth Ann was whining, "My flowers are all droopy."

"Let's go put them in water."

But the flowers didn't perk up. And Momma really would be home soon now and I hadn't started the mac and cheese.

This day wasn't working out like I'd planned.

Finally, I got Jackson "vrooming" with his trucks and Ruth Ann playing dress-up. I let her pick out a necklace from Momma's jewelry box. I lifted up the top tray to look underneath and way in the back, kind of crumpled, I saw an old photograph. I pulled it out.

"Is that my daddy?" asked Ruth Ann.

It didn't look like Tommy, but it was a boy about his age. Dark hair, standing by a blue truck. A pickup truck.

My heart started bouncing around. I stuffed the photo in my jeans.

"No," I said. "Which necklace do you want?"

"The yellow one," she decided.

With them busy, I got water boiling and the counter set with the dandelions in the middle. When the noodles were done, I mixed in the milk and cheese like the directions said. I was ready. Momma would be so happy when she got home and saw supper all ready.

A minute later, she walked in. She looked terrible. Her uniform was covered with spots, her hair was frizzed up, and her face was all blotchy.

"You won't believe the day I've had!" she said. "Juanita didn't show up and I had to do everything and then some kid spilled syrup all over my uniform and it got tracked on the floor and Frankie was yelling like it was my fault. And my head's about to split open!"

That sounded awful. But I'd make her feel better.

"I'm sorry, Momma," I said, sweet as could be. "But look, I fixed supper."

Momma didn't look happy like she was supposed to.

"You fixed supper? But I brought supper." She plunked down a bag. "Take-out chicken."

I hadn't thought of her doing that.

"I made mac and cheese," I said. "It's all ready."

"Well, you should have told me," Momma snapped. "How was I supposed to know?"

"It was a surprise," I mumbled.

Momma pressed her fingers against her forehead. "So now we've got two suppers. We'll just have to save the mac and cheese for tomorrow."

"But I love mac and cheese!" Ruth Ann squealed.

"Cheese!" said Jackson.

Momma looked beaten down. "Oh, alright. We'll have both."

It was the best supper we'd had in practically forever. Even Momma calmed down, chewing on a chicken leg.

"Do you like the flowers I picked for you?" asked Ruth Ann.

"They're real pretty, honey," said Momma.

What? Those flowers were my idea, not Ruth

Ann's. And Momma hadn't said anything about my mac and cheese. I couldn't help it. I had to ask.

"Very good," she said. "I didn't know you could cook, Weezie."

"It was easy. I just followed the directions on the box."

Momma's face brightened. "Well then, maybe you could do some more cooking. You know how hard I work every day."

This being-good thing was a big bust. Momma hadn't noticed the picked-up trailer, she thought the flowers were Ruth Ann's idea, and she'd brought home supper after I'd made it. Instead of making her happy, I'd just gotten myself another job.

She was waiting for me to answer.

"Yes, Momma. I could do that."

I washed the dishes while Momma dried. That mac and cheese pan was really sticky. I scrubbed till my fingers about fell off, then dried my hands on my jeans.

And felt the photograph in my pocket.

I had to look at it again. Right this minute.

I handed the pan to Momma.

"I'm going to do my homework," I told her. And went to my room.

The Truck Stop

I didn't start my homework. Instead, I took out the photograph. The colors were all faded and it was so old, it was cracked. Still, I could make out the boy and the truck. He looked about eighteen, same age as Tommy when he and Momma got married. Dark hair flopped over his forehead and a little smile on his face.

His hand was on the door of the truck, like he'd just gotten it and was feeling proud. The pickup was light blue and kind of old. Just like Uncle Billy said. This had to be my daddy!

He had a thin face like mine, and brown hair.

I couldn't see the color of his eyes. Or make out where he was.

I turned the picture over. In the corner was some smudged writing. "W" and "A." I held the photo closer to the lamp. "D" and then "E." W-A-D-E. My daddy's name was Wade! Under that, written small, was "Smoke." Was that his last name? His nickname? The name of his truck?

Anyway, I had some clues now. A photograph and a name—two names really. They could help me find my daddy. But how?

Right off I knew the answer. On TV, detectives were always showing pictures of who they thought did the crime. My daddy drove a truck. I was pretty sure of it now. I could show his picture to the drivers of those big rigs at the truck stop. Maybe they'd know him.

I'd do it right away, on Saturday!

Calvin liked my idea. I wasn't sure he understood about my daddy's picture, but he was happy to go to the truck stop. He was almost as crazy about trucks as cars.

It was a long ride out there. Calvin was huffing and puffing.

"Want me to get off and walk?" I offered.

"I—can—make—it," he puffed. Another good thing about Calvin, he never gave up. He'd keep pedaling till he fell right off his bike.

Finally we got there. Four big rigs were parked outside the Hot Biscuit Diner, and another was just pulling in. I headed for the nearest truck, a tall red one. I could see the driver inside, eating his lunch.

"Mister!" I said, waving my arms.

He didn't hear me, his Walkman radio attached to his ear. What if that actually was my daddy sitting there? And he didn't know his little girl was waving at him.

"THWEET!" Calvin let go his loudest whistle.

The window rolled down. "Hey, kids, what's up?"

Well, this couldn't be my daddy. He had gray hair. And a porcupine beard you know would hurt if you touched it.

"Uh, we're looking for someone," I said. "A truck driver. I wonder if you've seen him. Here's his picture."

I climbed the tall step and handed it to him. "His name is Wade. Or maybe Smoke."

The driver studied the photo, then shook his head. "I know a lot of truckers, but I can't say I know him. But this is an old picture. He may have changed some."

I hadn't thought of that. My daddy'd be around ten years older now.

"Sorry. But you could try some of the other drivers."

Calvin was standing on tiptoe, trying to see inside the truck.

"You like trucks?" the driver asked.

Calvin bobbed his head, his tongue practically hanging out.

"Well, climb in, both of you."

The inside was like a little house, full of stuff to eat and tools and photos of little kids. And behind the seat, the biggest surprise. A bed.

"Do you live in this truck?" I asked.

The driver laughed. "Just about. Spend more time in it than my house. My name's Tom Wiley, from Memphis."

"I'm Grace Louise, and this is Calvin. He doesn't talk much, but he likes your truck."

"Then he should sit in the driver's seat."

Tom Wiley showed Calvin everything on the fancy dashboard and let him work the windows that went up and down if you pressed a button. We never saw those before. Calvin's eyes lit up like Christmas. And all the time I was thinking this must be how my daddy lived. It looked like fun.

"Well, kids," Tom Wiley said, "I better hit the road. Hope you find that fella you're looking for. Relative of yours?"

"My daddy," I said.

"Oh, you do want to find him. Try some other drivers."

"Okay. Thanks, Mr. Wiley."

We watched him pull out. He tooted his horn, and Calvin grinned so wide, it looked like his face might break.

"You know what I'm going to be when I grow up?"

I could never guess. "A trucker?"

"Yep. I'm going to get me a big rig like that."

"Good plan," I told him.

But now we had to get back to my plan. We went over to the next truck, a silver tanker. I showed the driver the photo.

He shook his head. "Nope, never saw him."

The next driver was asleep. It didn't seem right to wake him up. And the other rigs were empty. The drivers must be having lunch in the diner.

"Let's go inside," I said. "I bet they have donuts in there." Donuts were Calvin's favorites.

"Okay," he said.

Calvin climbed right up on a stool, peering into the donut jar. I looked down the row of booths. Near the end were two men in ball caps. One said "King Oil." They had to be truckers. The waitress was filling their coffee cups.

"Uh, excuse me," I said, taking out the picture.

The men looked up. The waitress turned around.

"Weezie!" she said.

Uh-oh. It was Momma's friend, Billie Jo. I didn't know she worked at the diner. Quick, I stuffed the picture in my pocket.

"What are you doing here?" she asked.

Billy Jo had the loudest voice, loud as her streaked blond hair and bright red lipstick. People started staring.

"I just came out with Calvin," I said. "He likes to look at trucks."

"Well, you're awful far from home. Does your momma know you're out here? And talking to strangers? No offense, boys."

"She said it was okay," I said. "I was just going to ask them about their trucks. For Calvin."

I was never going to tell lies again, and here I was piling them on. Momma wouldn't say it was okay. She was always telling Ruth Ann not to talk to strangers. That must mean me too.

Billy Jo shook her head. "I don't know. If I was Charlene, I wouldn't want you at a truck stop. Didn't she hear about that kidnapping over in Ponca City? Little girl about your age. You better go on home."

Just about everyone was staring now, nodding as if they agreed.

"Okay," I said. "We're finished looking at trucks anyway."

"Bye then. And Weezie, say hello to your momma."

I had to practically drag Calvin out of there.

"I didn't finish my donut!" he protested.

"Take it with you."

The ride home seemed even longer. Calvin pumped slower and slower till finally we both got off and walked.

"Which one should I get?" he asked after a while.

"What?"

I was thinking about how Mr. Wiley didn't know my daddy even though he knew a lot of truckers, and neither did that other driver. Could that mean maybe he wasn't a trucker? And how could I go out there again with Billy Jo there? Next time she'd likely call Momma.

"Should I get a red truck or a silver one?"

"Oh. I like the red."

"Me too. I guess I'll take the red."

56

Finally, we got to the trailer park.

"See ya later, Refrigerator," I said, and he grinned.

I pushed open the trailer door and there was Momma, hands on hips, a major frown on her face. Uh-oh.

"Where have you been?" she asked in her quiet voice.

"Out riding with Calvin," I said.

"Riding where?"

"Just around."

"That's a lie!" she snapped. "I know where you've been. Out at that diner by the highway where the truckers hang out. Who said you could do that? And what were you doing there anyway?"

I knew it now. Billy Jo had called Momma.

"Just looking at trucks," I mumbled. "Calvin likes them."

There I went, lying some more.

"You know I'd never let you go out there. No telling what could happen to you, fooling around with those truckers." Her voice was rising. "What else have you been doing behind my back?"

I couldn't answer.

She didn't notice, just kept yelling. "I swear, you don't have a lick of sense, just like your friend Calvin. Well, you won't be going out there again, that's for sure. You won't be going anywhere for a good long time!"

Her words washed over me like pouring rain. I was drowning in them.

"Well," she said finally, quieting down. "Do you have anything to say for yourself?"

What could I say? Momma wouldn't believe me anyway.

I looked down at the floor. "No, Momma," I mumbled.

Prisoner

Momma meant it. I wasn't going anywhere ever again. I'd be a prisoner in the trailer forever. Taking care of Ruth Ann and Jackson. Making supper now that Momma had brought home six more boxes of macaroni and cheese. And doing nothing all day Saturday.

Calvin couldn't come over. I wasn't even supposed to talk to him because he was bad like me.

"Those quiet ones," Momma said. "You know they're up to something."

Which showed how much she knew about Calvin.

One good thing, though. She hadn't found out about the photograph. I kept it in my jeans pocket and kept looking at it till I knew I would never forget my daddy's face. Then I got to worrying Momma would find it when she did the laundry. So I hid it under my mattress.

Going nowhere during the week was no different than usual. I had to watch Ruth Ann and Jackson after school anyway. But Saturdays were bad.

Now that it was getting warmer, Momma took Ruth Ann and Jackson to the park where the nice swings were or Taco Bell or the 99 Cents Store and I had to stay home. And would you believe it, she had Mrs. Holcomb watching me! She didn't say so, but if I came outside because there was nothing to do inside, I'd see her curtain move. I was a prisoner with a little-old-lady guard.

I was sitting outside the second Saturday. Momma had taken Ruth Ann and Jackson to the Spring Fair at Eternal Life Church. They had rides there and everything. I'd like to have gone on those. I'd hold Jackson tight so he wouldn't get scared.

"Hi, Weezie." Calvin skidded to a stop in a cloud of dust.

"Hi," I said. Sure enough, Mrs. Holcomb's curtain moved.

"What're you doing?"

"Nothing. And you know I'm not allowed to talk to you."

He looked all hurt. No matter how many times I told him about Momma, he didn't seem to understand. Friends talked to friends, he thought.

"I'm not mad," I said. "It's my punishment. So you better go. Did you know there's a fair at Eternal Life Church? You could ride over."

Calvin brightened up. "Okay."

"See ya later, Elevator," I said, and he rode off grinning.

I was alone again. I looked at the bright yellow daffodils growing by Mrs. Holcomb's door. I wished we could have some, but I wouldn't dare ask Momma. She'd say we didn't have money for fancy doodads, I should know that.

The door opened and Mrs. Holcomb stepped out.

"Why, hello, Weezie," she said, as if she didn't already know I was there.

"Your flowers are real pretty," I said.

"Thank you. Daffodils are so happy-looking, aren't they?"

I hadn't thought of that, but they were.

"I'm going to Dora Lee's to have my hair done. I won't be gone long. You be good now."

That sounded like a warning. My prison guard would be back soon so I better not try to escape. Well, she didn't have to worry. I wasn't about to get in more trouble.

Everybody but me was doing something. The day stretched ahead of me forever. What could I do? I stared at the daffodils. Maybe I'd draw a picture of them. If it came out okay, I could give it to Mrs. Holcomb. She was nice even if she was my prison guard. I got my notebook and Ruth Ann's box of crayons.

The stems and leaves were easy, but not the flowers. My first one looked like a sun. I scrunched up the paper and tried again. Finally I got a daffodil that looked pretty good. I held it up to see if it matched the real ones.

Something bigger than a flower, but yellow too, was sitting in the middle of Mrs. Holcomb's daffodils. It was that cat that always hung around here looking for mice. That would make a nice picture.

It sat so still, its whiskers didn't even move, like it was posing for me. I drew its head, then tried to get the shape of its body. I was working on the tail when all of a sudden it stretched, shook its whiskers, and strolled out of the daffodils.

"Oh," I said.

The cat looked at me. I looked at the cat.

What do you say to a cat? Would you please go back where you were so I can draw you?

I know cats don't do what they're told. Specially cats like this one. It had a squashed-in face and one chewed ear, like it had been in a few fights. And it always acted like a big-shot, strutting around with its head held high like it owned the place. I liked that. The way it just did what it wanted, roaming free. In a crazy way, I kind of wished I was that cat.

"Hi, Cat," I said real quiet so as not to scare it off.

Uh-oh. That was the wrong move. The cat gave me a look like *I'm not talking to you* and ambled away.

How could I get it back? I really wanted to finish my picture. Plus it would be nice to have company, even if it was only a cat.

Food! I thought.

I ran inside and looked up on the shelf. What do cats like to eat? Peanut butter? Fruit Loops? Maybe not. I looked in the refrigerator. Hot dogs? No. Milk! That was it. I poured some in a saucer and took it outside.

"Here, Cat!" I called. "I have milk for you."

No yellow cat appeared.

Well, maybe if I left it out, the cat would smell it and come back. I picked up my cat picture and tried to work on the tail some more. But I couldn't get it right. I needed that cat to come back and pose for me.

A car came up the hill. It was Mrs. Holcomb, back from Dora Lee's.

"Your hair looks nice," I told her. It really did.

Mrs. Holcomb fluffed out the sides. "I always tell Dora Lee she's a whiz with hair. What have you been doing, drawing pictures?"

I held up the daffodil one. "I made this for you."

"Why, thank you, Weezie," she said.

"I was trying to draw that yellow cat, too," I said. "You know the one that's always hanging around here?"

"Oh, that stray. It doesn't belong to anyone. It's kind of wild. Well, I better get inside. Muffy'll be waiting for her doggy treat."

But she didn't go inside. She looked like she wanted to say something.

"Your momma," she said finally. "She's had a hard time. Losing her own momma, and then Tommy right after that. It just about broke her heart. He was going to build a house for her, you know, when he got back from the army."

I didn't know that.

"Anyway, I just wanted to say I'm sure you didn't do anything really bad. You're a real sweet girl."

Sweet girl—that's not what Momma thinks.

"You remember that, hear?" She smiled, holding up the daffodil picture.

It was hard to get the words out, but finally I did.

"Okay," I said. "I will."

The Yellow Cat

The next morning the milk was gone. That cat must have come back in the night.

So I put out more, in the weeds where Momma wouldn't notice and tell me I was wasting milk. The saucer was empty the next day, too. But I didn't see the cat anywhere. Not till three days later.

I was sitting on the front step, waiting for Ruth Ann and Jackson to come home. The first thing I saw was the tall grass moving. Like with the wind, only it wasn't windy. Then I caught a flash of yellow. I sat still, hardly breathing. Yes! It was my cat.

Well, of course it wasn't mine. But I kind of wished it was.

I watched as it wove through the grass, leaving a thin, green trail of ripples behind. Suddenly it stopped and crouched down. It stayed that way for the longest time. Then, so quick I didn't see it happen, it pounced.

A mouse—it had to be! The cat lifted its head and I could see it had something mouse-size in its mouth. Just like on my nature programs on TV. If I squinted my eyes, the tall grass could have been in Africa and the cat could have been a lion.

"Nice job, Cat," I said softly.

The cat paid no attention to me. With its head high, it strolled through the grass and disappeared.

No wonder that cat looked kind of beat-up. It must be hard having to hunt for your food. One time I saw it sneaking up on some birds. Just like today, it crept closer and closer. Then, just as it was about to pounce, the birds flew away.

Mrs. Holcomb said it was wild. But maybe if I gave it food and got it used to having me around, I could tame it. I could get it to be my friend.

For the next few days, I kept putting out milk, and the milk kept disappearing. I knew milk wasn't enough, though. What else could I feed it?

I looked on the shelf again. Nothing but boxes of cereal and macaroni and cheese and canned stuff.

That was no good. I popped the lid of the garbage can. It smelled fishy inside. Oh, cats liked fish! I dug down and found a tuna fish can. It was empty, but still had some juice and little bits at the bottom.

I set it out in the weeds. The next morning, it was licked clean.

That gave me an idea. Ruth Ann never finished anything on her plate. After supper, Momma scraped it off into the garbage. So whatever I found there, I started putting out for the cat. Spaghetti-Os, chicken nuggets, mac and cheese.

The cat ate it all.

I asked Momma to buy more tuna.

"I didn't know you liked it that much," she said.

"I *love* tuna," I said, just like Ruth Ann always said she loved Tootsie Pops.

So I got another tuna can for the cat.

Still, it only came at night. I hadn't seen it in the daytime since it caught that mouse.

One afternoon I put out a few French fries. I wasn't sure cats liked potatoes but they were all I had. As I came back to my step, I caught a glimpse of the cat lurking in the bushes. Like it was waiting for its meal.

The cat walked in circles, as if it wasn't sure

what to do. It had never come for food while I was sitting right there. It must be really hungry. It came a little closer, then sat down to think about it some more. And then it crouched down by the plate of French fries.

"You did it, Cat!" I said, but only to myself. I wasn't about to scare it off.

The cat sniffed at the fries. It wasn't too sure about them, probably wishing they were tuna. But then it started eating. I'd done it. I'd tamed that cat! Not all the way, of course, but it was a start. Pretty soon I'd have it sitting in my lap.

I couldn't just keep calling it Cat. I needed to give it a name. Tiger, maybe? Or Daisy, because it was yellow? That sounded like a girl cat and I didn't know if it was.

Suddenly the perfect name popped into my head. Perfect because it came from Gramma Emmeline. She had a favorite jam she used to spread on her breakfast toast. It was orangey-yellow. Marmalade, she called it.

"Marmalade," I said in my quietest voice. "That's what I'm going to call you."

I sat there feeling good inside, watching my tamed cat finish off those French fries. A minute later, Mrs.

Atchley's car came chugging up the hill. And when I looked again, Marmalade had disappeared.

"Oh," I said out loud.

I guessed I hadn't quite tamed it yet. But I'd do it. I would.

A Liar and a Cheat

I couldn't stop thinking about my daddy on account of his photograph. I kept looking at it every day. He seemed real to me now, as real as Tommy or Roy.

"I have a daddy too," I felt like saying to Ruth Ann when she talked about Tommy. "See? Here's his picture." But of course I couldn't do that. Then Momma would find out I had it.

Like Roy said, it wasn't natural not to know your own daddy. Why wouldn't Momma tell me about him? Why did I have to try to find him myself? Which was hard work, I'd found out already. At least she could tell me his name. Was it really Wade?

And Smoke—what did that mean? What was his last name?

If she'd just tell me that, maybe I could find him myself. I bet I could. I had to ask at the right time, though, when Momma was feeling good. No Ruth Ann whining, no headache, no Frankie bugging her.

After supper the next night, Momma was sitting with her feet up, reading one of her beauty magazines. She liked to look at the latest hairstyles that the Hollywood stars were wearing. She'd point out how this one's cut wasn't right for her long face, but that one's curls going all the way down her back were amazing. I guessed she still hadn't given up on having that salon with Marcella.

Everything was quiet. Jackson was playing with his army truck on the floor. Ruth Ann had one of his plastic soldiers, pretending it was Tommy.

"My daddy gets to sit up front 'cause he's the boss of the whole army," she announced.

Her daddy. She was so proud of him. Suddenly my question popped out all on its own.

"Momma," I said. "What's my daddy's name?"

She looked up from the magazine. "I've told you and told you, Weezie. You don't want to know about him."

She didn't seem mad. She thought I'd stop asking. But I wasn't going to. Not this time.

"Yes I do," I said. "I need to know about my daddy. Ruth Ann knows about hers and Jackson has a daddy right here in town. Where's mine?"

Momma put down her magazine.

"Well, he's nowhere around here, if that's what you're wondering. I don't know where he is and I don't care."

"But I care," I said right back. "At least I should know his name. Please, Momma. It's not right not to know your own daddy's name."

She was starting to get annoyed, I could tell. But what could she do to me? I was already a prisoner in the trailer.

"Your own daddy," she snapped. "You really want to know? All right, I'll tell you about your own daddy. He was no good! Your daddy was a liar and a cheat. A sneaking, thieving, no-account son of a—"

She broke off, pointing a finger at me.

"Listen to me, Weezie. You should count yourself lucky not to know your daddy. You never want to meet him. You know where he most likely is now? In jail!"

That couldn't be, I thought. Not that nice boy in the photograph.

"Now you know," Momma said, picking up her magazine again. "So you'll never have to ask about him again."

I hadn't gotten her to tell me his name. All I'd gotten was a bunch of bad stuff about him. Could all that be true?

That night I couldn't sleep. I just lay there with my eyes wide open. I kept hearing Momma's words and seeing my daddy's photograph in my head. Just because he looked nice didn't mean he was. I knew that. But could he be so bad he was in jail?

Being in jail would be awful—much worse than being a prisoner in the trailer. There'd be bars on the windows and guards with real guns, and you couldn't go outside except maybe once a week. Finally, I fell asleep. But then I dreamed there were bars on the windows of the trailer and Momma had gone off someplace and locked the door and I couldn't get out.

That woke me up. And then I thought of something else she said. My daddy told lies, and I told lies too. He might be in jail, and I was in jail now on Saturdays. My daddy and me, we both were bad.

Louella

"What's the matter with you, Weezie?"

Momma's voice pierced through the fog in my head.

"I called you three times! You're going to miss the bus."

I threw on my clothes, grabbed a piece of toast, and ran out the door. Sure enough, the bus was already at the bus stop. I plunked myself down next to Calvin. My head was so fuzzy, I didn't notice who was sitting behind us till she leaned over and whispered in my ear.

"Will we be seeing you and your daddy at the Easter egg hunt next Sunday?"

Ruby. Would she ever quit?

I wouldn't answer. That was my plan, I remembered.

"Hey, Calvin," I said. "Look at that red car! Bet you'd like one of those."

"Yep, I would," he said.

I kept talking. "I like blue. When I grow up, I'll have a blue car." The color of my daddy's truck, I was thinking.

"Hey!" It was Ruby again. "You didn't answer my question."

I ignored her.

"A convertible, I think. Or maybe one of those little sports cars."

I didn't stop talking about cars the rest of the way to school. Calvin looked confused. But Ruby finally shut up. At least until we got off the bus. She ran off, calling back, "See you next Sunday!"

My plan had worked pretty well. I just had to keep ignoring her till she got tired of bothering me and picked on someone else.

She hadn't given up, though.

"See you next Sunday!" she said in the cafeteria line at lunch. And again at Art. This time she just mouthed it, like we had some kind of secret.

"What's Ruby saying?" asked Louella Hitchins next to me.

"Oh, she just wants me to come to the Easter egg hunt at her church."

"Are you going?"

"Not with her."

"I wouldn't go with her either. She's such a pain."

This was the most I'd talked to Louella all year. She lives in Sunset Acres up on the hill where all the nice new houses are. Those girls don't talk much to us trailer kids.

Then Ms. Martinelli walked to the front of the class and held up a vase of spring flowers.

"What do you see?" she said. "What colors and shapes pop out at you? How do they make you feel?"

"Why do we have to draw dumb flowers?" asked a boy in back.

Ms. Martinelli just smiled. She was so different from our old art teacher. She was young, with curly black hair that always looked kind of wild. She dressed wild too. Long, flowery skirts and big hoop earrings and lots of bracelets that clinked together when she moved. No one knew where she came from, but I figured California or maybe New York City. She lived in a little house outside of town where she made crazy sculptures out of junk like old car parts and farm tools.

I liked her. The boys did too, I knew. They just liked to complain.

I stared at the flowers, half-closing my eyes to see what popped out at me. It was the daffodils. Bright yellow like Mrs. Holcomb's, with ruffly white centers. I picked out a yellow pencil and started drawing.

"That's so good!" said Louella.

I looked over at hers. She'd just drawn a circle.

"Yours is going to be good too."

"No it's not." Louella made a face. "I'm terrible at art."

"Quiet, girls," said Ms. Martinelli. "Let the flowers talk to you."

That sounded weird. But the more I looked, the more they did. The daffodils said they were happy. The tulips were soft and round. The irises poked up straight as flags, like they were saying, "Look at me!"

I used all my colored pencils trying to get the shapes and colors just right. The irises were the hardest. Their shapes were so strange.

"Time to clean up," said Ms. Martinelli.

I was surprised Art was over so soon. I wished I could keep going. But we had to put everything away.

"Mine is awful," said Louella. "It looks like a bunch of lollipops."

It did, really.

"But your daffodils look so great!"

"They do." Ms. Martinelli smiled at me. "You've captured them, Weezie."

"Uh—thanks," I said. "My irises aren't very good, though."

"You know," said Ms. Martinelli, "you don't have to copy them so they look exactly like the real ones. Art isn't about that. It's about how they look to you."

Really? Our old art teacher always wanted us to copy stuff.

"So maybe you haven't looked quite hard enough at the irises."

"Maybe."

She was looking me right in the eye now, not smiling. "Keep trying. I know you can do it."

That gave me a funny feeling. Did she really mean it?

Louella walked out the door with me.

"See?" she said. "Ms. Martinelli thinks you're good too."

She probably didn't. Probably she was just trying to be nice. Still, I felt a little bubble of something inside.

What was that?

Happy, I thought. I felt happy.

An Easter Rabbit

I was sitting outside again on the Saturday before Easter. Momma had taken Ruth Ann and Jackson to the 99 Cents Store to buy Easter candy and probably a whole lot of other stuff. Like anything Ruth Ann begged for. She always got what she wanted.

And here I was, still in prison. It looked like I'd never get out.

It was quiet. Calvin was down at Pinkerton Motors looking at cars. He still told me everything he was going to do, even though I couldn't go with him. And Mrs. Holcomb was grocery shopping. She wasn't really guarding me any more. She knew I wasn't running off anyplace.

One good thing, though. I could do some more drawing. Ever since Ms. Martinelli said what she said, I wanted to keep practicing. I started a new daffodil picture. That would be a nice surprise for Momma when she came home. Maybe then she'd notice I was trying hard to be good and release me from prison. Maybe.

At the same time, I was keeping an eye out for Marmalade. He was a boy cat, I'd decided, since he acted so tough. I had a plan for taming him. I'd seen it on one of my nature programs. This forest ranger tamed a bear cub by feeding it and talking to it. You had to go slow—that was the important thing. Little by little, talking real quiet, he got that bear to come closer and closer till he could touch him. And before you knew it, they were best friends.

That was how it was going to be with me and Marmalade.

I drew a whole row of happy-looking daffodils. "Happy Easter!" I wrote on the bottom. I put the picture inside on the refrigerator and came back out.

Something moved under Mrs. Holcomb's window. It was large and yellow. Marmalade!

Would he go off when he saw me or stay around? He stood still, like he wasn't sure. Then he jumped up the way cats do, like they have springs on their feet. He walked in a circle and sat down next to one of the pansy pots.

Now what? Should I talk to him? Maybe not yet. He seemed peaceful sitting in the sun. Then he curled himself into a ball and closed his eyes. It looked like he was asleep.

This was nice, the two of us together in a friendly way. I didn't dare move in case I'd wake him up. A song popped into my head. It was the one Momma used to sing to Jackson and Ruth Ann when they were babies. Maybe to me too. Who knows? I could kind of remember someone singing to me.

"Rockabye baby in the treetops. When the wind blows, the cradle will rock . . ."

I whispered the words, quiet as could be. Marmalade didn't move. So after a while, I whispered some other things.

"Marmalade—do you know that's your new name? Did you used to have another name? I bet you did. Why don't you belong to anyone? Would you like to belong to me?"

Well, that was a silly question. Momma would never let me have a cat in the trailer.

"Would you like to be my friend?"

That was better.

Marmalade's eyes were still closed. Could he hear

me even if he was sleeping? I wondered.

Something was coming up the hill. Too loud for a car. It had to be a motorcycle. *Roy,* I thought.

Why did he have to show up now? I looked up and Marmalade was gone. Disappeared into the air like a magic trick just when I was starting to get my plan going.

Roy coasted to a stop.

"Look what I brought Jackson," he said. "I told you I would."

It was an Easter rabbit. Not the soft, cuddly kind, though. This one was about as tall as Jackson with standing-up ears, wearing a little red jacket.

"So you got the job at 7-Eleven?" I said.

Roy looked at the ground. "No, I won it at the County Fair last fall."

I saw now that the rabbit wasn't new. One ear was bent and the jacket looked dusty. Still, it was nice of Roy to give Jackson an Easter rabbit.

"Do you think he'll like it?" His eyes looked all worried.

"Sure he will," I said. Which was kind of a lie. Jackson would like a truck a whole lot better.

Roy didn't look happy. In fact, he looked down in the dumps. He sat down next to me on the step.

"It's hard," he said. "I wanted to buy him something

special, like one of those little cars he could sit in and pedal himself. But I don't have any money because I can't get a job. And I can't get a decent job unless I go to trade school and I can't do that because I don't have any money."

It sounded like he was going in circles, getting nowhere.

"I want to be Jackson's daddy. I really do. Take him places and give him stuff. Teach him to ride a motorcycle when he's older. Only your momma makes it so tough, you know?"

I sure knew that. Roy would be a good daddy, I could tell. I felt bad for him.

"Well," I said. "At least you get to see Jackson a little bit." I stopped, wondering if I should say it. And then I did. "I never met my daddy at all."

Roy looked at me.

"Really? I didn't know that. Your momma used to talk about Tommy, but she never told me anything about your daddy."

She wouldn't. She hated him so much.

"Me neither," I said. "She won't even tell me his name."

It felt good to tell someone. Specially Roy, knowing how he felt about Jackson.

"Wow. That really stinks." He picked up some dirt

and let it fall through his fingers. "You poor kid. It looks like she's got us both stuck."

We sat there awhile, not saying anything.

"Uh-oh!" Roy jumped up. "That sounds like your momma's car. I better get out of here."

He hopped on his bike. "See you, Weezie. Don't forget the rabbit."

"I won't. Jackson will like it."

Momma's car stopped and she got out, slamming the door.

"What's he doing here?" she demanded.

"Just bringing Jackson an Easter present," I said. "See, it's a big rabbit."

"That snake!" she said. "Thinks he can worm his way into Jackson's life with presents when he doesn't give me a dime."

"He's trying to get a job," I said.

Oops, I should have kept my mouth shut.

"Hah!" She eyed the rabbit. "Where'd he get that, anyway? Steal it?"

Momma was working up to getting real mad. I better change the subject.

"Look, Jackson," I said. "It's a great big Easter bunny!"

Jackson didn't seem to care. "Pop," he said, holding out a Tootsie Pop. He had chocolate goo all over his face.

That wasn't right. Poor Roy was trying so hard to be a daddy. Jackson had to like his present. I'd make him like it.

Inside, I helped Momma unload her shopping bags.

"We got so much candy!" said Ruth Ann. "Jelly-beans and chocolate eggs and marshmallow chickens. And hair ribbons too!"

Jackson was down on the floor with his trucks. I sat next to him.

"Look at the nice bunny!" I said. "He's wearing a jacket just like you do."

Jackson went "vroom" with his oil truck.

"You can hug him, see?" I gave the rabbit a hug. "Now you give the bunny a big hug."

I pushed the rabbit at him. Jackson pushed it back so hard it fell over.

This wasn't working. I'd promised Roy he'd like that rabbit.

Jackson's big dump truck was loaded with maca-roni and cheese boxes. I dumped them out and tried to put the rabbit in. But he was too big.

I folded and scrunched his legs until finally I got him wedged in.

"Hey, Jackson, look!" I said. "You can take your bunny for a ride."

"Ride," he said.

He drove the rabbit—"vroom! vroom!"—all over the trailer, from the counter to the TV and all the way to his crib and back.

"Nice bunny," he said.

I'd done it! Jackson liked his daddy's Easter present.

Colored Pencils

Marmalade kept coming back just about every afternoon. I knew he was there for the food I left out, but maybe he was starting to be my friend, too.

He sat on Mrs. Holcomb's step like before and I talked to him. Quietly, like the man with the bear cub. I told him how handsome he was with that pretty yellow fur.

"But you could use a bath, if you don't mind my saying so. I could give you one sometime, maybe. What happened to your ear? Did you get into a fight? I bet you beat up whoever did it, you're so tough. So which do you like better, chicken nuggets or tuna?"

Of course, he didn't answer. But he didn't seem to mind. He didn't get up and walk away.

"Would it be okay if I drew a picture of you?" I asked one day.

Marmalade opened one eye and closed it again.

I took that for a yes. So I squinted at him, looking to see what popped out at me, like Ms. Martinelli said. It was the way he was curled up almost in a circle, tail wrapped around his front paws. Everything was round: the cat, the pot, and the pansies. Oh, that would make a super picture!

I worked really hard on it, and Marmalade didn't move one time till I was finished. Like he was happy to help me out. The picture came out pretty well, I thought. I stuck it in my backpack. Maybe I'd show it to Louella tomorrow.

It turned out I did, after we finished our flower pictures. My irises had come out better, so I felt kind of good.

"That's great!" Louella said. "Is it your cat?"

"No," I said. "It's just a stray that hangs around our place."

"You should show it to Ms. Martinelli," she said.

Ms. Martinelli heard her. "Show me what?"

So I had to show her, which made me feel like I was bragging or something.

She leaned over my desk, her red and yellow bracelets clinking. She didn't say anything for a long time. Just when I thought she was going to tell me nicely that I hadn't really looked at the cat enough, she said, "You've captured something, Weezie. What do you think it is?"

Me? She was the teacher. She was supposed to tell me.

"Uh, I think I got the shapes pretty well."

She nodded. "And something else. I feel the peacefulness of this cat."

I hadn't thought of that. He did look peaceful.

"I couldn't get the details right," I said. "All I have at home is crayons."

Ms. Martinelli ran her fingers through her hair, making it stand out like a dark cloud around her head. She did that a lot when she was thinking.

"It's not the details that matter," she said. "It's the feeling you put into your work. But crayons aren't the best medium, I agree. Why don't you take home a box of colored pencils? You can bring them back at the end of the year."

Really? I could do that?

"Okay," I said. "Thank you."

"Thank you for showing it to me, Weezie. You're doing good work."

Wow! That was something, coming from her.

Louella was waiting for me outside the art room. "What did she say? Did she like it?"

"Yes. She said the cat looked peaceful. And she let me borrow a box of colored pencils."

"You don't have any at home?"

Probably Louella had all kinds of art supplies at her house, seeing as she lived in Sunset Acres. All of a sudden I felt strange talking to her. But she didn't seem to care. She walked with me to the cafeteria and I sat down at a table with her without even thinking about it.

Louella kept talking about art. It was what she most wanted to be good at, but she wasn't.

"I'm okay at piano," she said. "And my ballet teacher thought I was good, but I hated it. I know— maybe you could teach me! You could come to my house after school and we could draw together. You could draw my dog."

I was surprised she'd invite me to her house. But of course I couldn't go.

"I have to take care of my little sister and brother after school," I said.

"Well, maybe Saturday then."

I didn't know what to say to that. I couldn't tell her I was a prisoner on Saturdays.

"Maybe," I said finally.

"Oh, let's do it!" Louella seemed excited. "I'll have my momma call yours, okay? This will be fun!"

It would be if it ever happened. But Momma would never let me out of prison.

Still, I had the colored pencils. That was something. And Ms. Martinelli liked my cat picture. And it seemed like Louella wanted to be my friend.

It had been a good day.

Drawing Roxie

Louella's momma called the next day to ask if I could come to her house on Saturday. And the strange thing was that Momma said yes.

I couldn't understand it. I thought I'd be in prison forever, and suddenly I was free. How did that happen? But in the car on the way over, Momma said, "Sounds like this Louella is a nice girl. Her daddy has that insurance office downtown. Better to be friends with her than that Calvin."

Oh, that was it. She still thought Calvin was some kind of criminal.

She let me out in front of Louella's house.

"Now you act nice with these people," she said.

Louella's house was long and low, like three trailers strung together, but nicer. It was white with blue shutters and some kind of trellis thing with roses climbing on it. Nice and neat.

Louella opened the door before I could ring the bell. Her momma was right behind her.

"We're so glad you could come," she said with a big smile.

Mrs. Hitchins looked exactly like Louella. Same round face and dark, curly hair and the same way of talking, all bubbly.

"Louella told us what a wonderful artist you are!"

"Yes, ma'am," I said. "I mean, I'm not that good."

"Yes she is," said Louella. "You should see the cat picture she drew."

"I'd love to sometime," Mrs. Hitchins said. "But I know you girls want to get started on new pictures. I'll see you later."

I followed Louella down a long hall, past a fancy dining room like you'd see on TV, and a bedroom with pink flower curtains. At the end was a closed door.

"Get ready," said Louella. "You're about to meet Roxie."

All of a sudden a little white dog was bouncing all over the place, barking, jumping, and wagging its tail like crazy. It was like Mrs. Holcomb's dog only with curly hair and lots more energy.

"Momma hates it when she does that," said Louella. "That's why I have to close her in my room when company comes."

"Hi, Roxie," I said.

That got her jumping up, trying to lick my face.

"Down, Roxie!" said Louella. "See? She pays no attention to me. She's real smart, but I guess she's spoiled."

Roxie raced to a corner and raced back with a yellow rubber bone.

"Oh, she wants you to throw it for her. Lie down, Roxie!"

Of course she didn't.

"Just ignore her," said Louella. "She'll get tired after a while and then we can draw her."

I looked around the room. Flowers were on every-thing: the curtains, a chair, the tall bed. I'd never seen a bed like that. It had wood posts at the corners and a ruffly white roof on top. It was so high you had to climb on a stool to get up on it.

"Your bed is real nice," I said.

"It was my momma's when she was little. It's called a four-poster. You can sit on it if you want. I'll get out the drawing stuff."

I climbed up, leaned on the fat pillows, and looked up at the pretty roof. I felt like a princess. Oh, I'd like a bed like this. In a room of my own.

"I think Roxie's quieting down now," said Louella.

She'd taken out all kinds of art supplies. Pads of real art paper, drawing pencils, watercolor paints like we had at school. She even had an easel.

Maybe it was rude, but I had to ask. "Where did you get all this stuff?"

"From my daddy," she said. "His momma, my gramma, was an artist and he wants me to be one, too. So he keeps giving me art stuff. See that picture by the bed? My gramma painted it."

It was of a flower garden, soft and misty like things look after it rains. I wished I could make a picture like that.

"That's really pretty," I said.

"So what do you want to start with?"

"Let's just use pencils. And can we use that art paper?"

"Sure." She climbed up next to me.

This was something, sitting up on Louella's princess bed with a whole pad of nice, smooth drawing paper. If you messed up, you just threw that piece away. And if you used up the whole pad, your daddy bought you another one.

"How should we start?" Louella asked.

I looked at Roxie, curled up now in the flower chair.

"Squint your eyes," I said. "See what about Roxie pops out at you."

Roxie's ears pricked up. She jumped down, picked up the yellow bone, and raced over to the bed.

"You said her name," said Louella. "She thinks you want to play."

"Oh no!" I said. "Sorry."

"That's okay. Just don't move or say her name again and she'll give up."

Sure enough, Roxie went back to the chair. But a minute later, she jumped down and ran to the window, barking.

"What's wrong now?"

"Squirrels. She hates them."

I had to laugh. "Your dog is crazy."

That's the way it went all afternoon. We'd start drawing, then Roxie would be barking out the window or sitting by the bed with begging eyes, like, "Play with me!" I tried to make quick sketches of her moving, while Louella just kept drawing circles and getting upset.

Finally she said, "You know what? R-o-x-i-e is not a good subject."

"No," I said. "Not like those flowers at school. R-o-x-i-e would never make it in Ms. Martinelli's class."

"Poor R-o-x-i-e! She'll never get to go to school."

As if she knew what we were saying, Roxie barked. That got us laughing.

"Where did R-o-x-i-e get her name?" I asked.

"My momma named her after some country singer. She said she looked like her and sounded like her too."

Louella leaned back against the pillows. "Where'd you get the name Weezie?"

"Oh, that's not my real name. My name is Grace Louise but my little sister couldn't say it, so I got to be Weezie."

"You're so lucky to have a sister and brother. I'm an only. My name came from my daddy, Louis, and my momma, Ella. They put them together to make Louella."

That was so nice. Her momma and daddy must really love each other to do that.

"Hey," said Louella. "Want a snack?"

"Sure."

Roxie tried to follow us, but Louella closed the door on her.

"You should see her beg if I let her in the kitchen. It's disgusting!"

The kitchen was so big. Our whole trailer would practically fit inside it. It had flower curtains, of course. Yellow daisies this time. And it smelled like cookies. Mrs. Hitchins was just taking them out of the oven.

"I thought you girls might like some fresh-baked cookies," she said. "They're healthy—oatmeal raisin—if your momma fusses about that."

"No, ma'am," I said. "She doesn't fuss."

Momma didn't care what we ate as long as it didn't cost much.

Mrs. Hitchins poured us glasses of milk, then sat down at the table.

"How did the drawing go?" she asked.

"Terrible," said Louella. "Roxie wouldn't stay still."

Mrs. Hitchins laughed. "I'm not surprised. That little dog is precious, but she's always into some thing. Do you have any pets, Weezie?"

I thought of Marmalade. But he wasn't really a pet. Or mine either.

"No, ma'am," I said. "It's too crowded in the trailer already."

"Oh, that's right. You live out at Happy Days, don't you? My, they have some cute trailer homes! It must be fun to live there."

Did she mean that? She seemed kind of excited about it. Not like most people in town, who I'd heard called us trailer trash. And I'd never say our trailer was cute. Maybe she'd seen Mrs. Holcomb's.

"And the best thing is, you can just hitch up your trailer and go any place you want. Does your daddy ever talk about doing that?"

"Uh—" I stopped. What could I say about my daddy? Did Louella know about the lies I'd told Ruby? Should I say the same ones?

They were both looking at me. I had to say something.

"Uh," I said again. "I don't have a daddy."

"Oh. Well, I'm sorry to hear that." Mrs. Hitchins reached over and squeezed my hand. She was so nice, I thought.

And Mr. Hitchins too. He came in, bald-headed and smiling, carrying a curtain rod. He shook my hand and kissed Louella's cheek.

"Now where are those works of art I've been hearing about?" he asked.

So we had to get our art pads to show him.

Mr. Hitchins looked carefully at my squiggles and Louella's circles.

"You've got some good movement going there," he said to me. "And Louella, if that dog ever lies still, you'll have a winner."

Louella was happy, I could see.

"Want a cookie, Daddy?" she asked.

"Well, of course."

He sat down and we all had more cookies. They were still warm. And that kitchen, with its daisy curtains and Louella and her nice momma and daddy, seemed like about the best place I could be.

A Blue Pickup Truck

Ruby was like a mosquito. You swat and swat at it, but it won't go away. It keeps coming back and buzzing in your ear.

"How's your daddy?" was her latest.

She buzzed it in my ear going to school and going home. I tried to ignore it, but that didn't stop the buzzing. Finally I heard myself say, "He's good."

Now why'd I go and say that? It was the dumbest thing I could do.

Ruby leaned over the aisle. "Is he coming home for Memorial Day? Are you taking him to the parade?"

I didn't answer.

"Huh? What's the matter? Can't talk?"

I shut my mouth tight so no words would come out.

Finally it worked. She stared at me another minute, then started rolling a spitball to throw at Bobby Flick.

That's when Calvin poked me in the ribs.

"Look-it that," he said.

It was just a pickup passing the bus. Light blue, kind of old.

Oh! If that didn't look just like the pickup in my daddy's picture! I stretched to see it better. All I could make out was the back end. The tailpipe was all rusty.

It couldn't be the same one. There must be lots of pickups that color. And why would my daddy still be riding around in the one he used to have?

But what if it was? What if he'd come back to take me away, just like in my dreams?

My stomach felt jumpy, like I'd eaten something bad for lunch.

"Did you see the driver?" I asked

"Nope."

The truck was pulling away. If only Mrs. Pinto would go faster. Instead, she slowed down around a curve and the blue truck was gone. Disappeared like it had never been.

But I'd seen it. Calvin had too. Then I had another thought. What if my daddy was waiting for me right now at the trailer?

At our stop I said, "See ya later, Radiator!" and started running. Past old Mr. Leach in his lawn chair, past Bobby's bike leaning against Mrs. Atchley's mailbox, down the road till I could see our trailer.

No blue truck was sitting outside.

Slowly I walked the rest of the way. That was that. It hadn't been my daddy, just some old blue pickup passing by. I sat down on the front step and looked for Marmalade. I could tell him about it. But he wasn't anywhere around.

All of a sudden I thought of something else. What if my daddy had come to town but he didn't know about us living at Happy Days and he went to Gramma Emmeline's house instead?

I needed to go there. And the funniest thing, I looked up and there was Calvin waiting to take me. Sometimes his head worked pretty good.

"You think it was him?" he asked.

"I don't know, but we have to get to town."

Have you ever noticed how when you can't wait to get someplace, time slows down? Calvin was pedaling hard like always, but it felt like a turtle could pass us by.

After about a hundred years, we got to the Mobil station where Roy used to work. Suddenly Calvin stopped.

I poked his back. "What're you stopping for?"

He pointed at that same blue truck, just pulling out of the station.

My heart did a great big skip.

"Follow that truck!" I said just like on TV.

Calvin tried, but then a black car pulled between us and the truck. I was trying to see who the driver was but I couldn't because of that car, and Calvin was trying to pass it, and then we came to the only stoplight in town. And wouldn't you know, it turned red just then.

Calvin stepped hard on the brakes. I bounced in the air—and came down hard on my backside, right in the middle of Main Street.

"Are you okay?"

A couple of old ladies came rushing toward us. I had a pain in my backside and my elbow too, but I had to get up. We couldn't lose that truck.

"I'm fine," I called and climbed back on the bike.

Had we lost it? I couldn't see the truck, and then I did. Parked between Dora Lee's House of Beauty and the Star Drugstore.

"Stop!" I said.

No one was in the truck. The driver couldn't be at Dora Lee's, so he must be in the drugstore. I ran inside. No one was there but the druggist, Mr. Veezey. I waved and ran out again.

He must be someplace else. Across the street, McCreery's Hardware was having a spring sale. Lawn-mowers and grass seed bags were lined up outside.

"Come on," I said to Calvin.

McCreery's was crowded with men. My stomach did that jumping thing again. Could one of them be my daddy? He was older now, but he'd still have his dark hair. So it wasn't the red-headed guy at the register. Or the fat one in the O.U. sweatshirt. My daddy couldn't be fat.

Down the tool aisle I saw a tall man, kind of thin. He looked pretty young. I couldn't tell about his hair because he was wearing a ball cap. That might be him, I thought. But I needed to get closer.

"Are we going to tail him?" Calvin whispered loudly.

He loved cop shows, on account of the car chases. I wasn't sure about him tailing someone, though. He wasn't real good at sneaking around.

"Maybe we should split up," I said. "So we can cover the whole store."

"Okay."

He went off and I wandered down the aisle. The man was by the power tools. I pretended to look at screwdrivers. Lordy me, as Gramma Emmeline used to say, they sure had a lot of different kinds. How did people choose?

I stole a peek at the man. He wore faded jeans and a jean jacket, muddy boots, and that cap that pretty much covered his face.

I took a step closer.

"Sure is hard to make up your mind, isn't it?"

He was talking. To me! I turned and saw him smiling, the cap pushed back now. He had a lined face and dark hair sprinkled with gray.

This couldn't be my daddy. He was old. Fifty, at least.

"Y-yes," I got out.

Just then I heard Calvin's voice, high and squeaky, coming from the front of the store. And another, deeper one.

"Hey, boy! Leave me alone!"

"Gotta go," I mumbled and ran up front.

Calvin had hold of a skinny little man in overalls.

"I just asked you," he kept saying.

"Yeah. Five times. No, that ain't my truck out there."

"Calvin," I said. "It's okay. Let's go now."

But Calvin wasn't about to quit. He'd tailed this guy and now he was giving him the police interrogation.

"Are you that girl's daddy?" he demanded.

Oh, lordy me. It was bad enough, Calvin up and accusing some guy of being my daddy. But those greasy overalls had "Crowley's Garage" printed across the front. He was Ruby's daddy!

"I'm sorry," I said. "He's a little mixed up."

"Looks like it," he muttered and about ran out the door.

Mr. McCreery was giving us a funny look. We better leave before Calvin got us arrested or something.

I dragged him outside.

"Where are we going?"

"Home."

Then I stopped short. The blue truck was still across the street, but now it was moving. Past the bank and Drucker's Dry Cleaning and the Harmony Theater. And turning in at Pinkerton Motors.

We both started to run. At the car dealer I stopped. Where was the truck? All I saw was a line of shiny new cars.

A man came toward us. "Calvin! What can I sell you today? The '88s are looking good!"

This must be Mr. Pinkerton. Of course he knew Calvin, he hung out there so much.

"We're looking for the old truck that just turned in here," I said.

"Oh, that would be our service department. Just through that door."

Right away I saw the blue truck parked outside.

"Where can we find the driver of that truck?" I asked the blond guy at the counter.

"He's in the waiting room."

Finally we'd caught up to him. My stomach started doing flip-flops.

I opened the door. No one was there but a real old man reading a hunting magazine. Bent over, with wispy white hair, he looked as old as Uncle Billy.

"That's not your daddy," said Calvin.

It sure wasn't. We walked back to the counter.

"There's only one man in there. A real old guy."

"That's George Foster," said the blond guy. "Mr. Pinkerton keeps telling him he should trade in that truck for a new one, but he won't do it. He loves that old truck. So what're you gonna do?"

I couldn't believe it. All this time we'd been chasing that truck, and it turned out to belong to some old geezer.

I was wasting my time. I'd never find my daddy.

"Come on, Calvin," I said. "Let's go home."

Peanut Butter Cookies

"What do you do over at that Louella's house anyway?"

Momma was looking at me with eyes that said it must be something bad.

I couldn't think what that could be. I hadn't even told any lies lately.

"Uh," I said. "Mostly we draw pictures."

Her eyebrows came down.

"What do you want to do that for? Drawing pictures never did anyone any good. It'll never help pay the rent, that's for sure."

I didn't know what to say to that. Drawing pictures

made me feel good, that was all. But I guessed Momma was right about it not paying the rent.

"And we play with her dog, Roxie," I said, "and her momma lets us help make cookies."

Momma frowned. "You could make cookies here. Ruth Ann loves cookies."

Why was Momma acting like this? I thought she wanted me to have a new friend so I wouldn't be with that bad Calvin all the time. Now that I had Louella for a friend, she still wasn't satisfied. Did she maybe think I liked it better at Louella's house than our trailer? Was that why she was being so cranky?

I couldn't tell Momma, but sometimes I did like it better there. It was so quiet at Louella's house. Nobody yelled and Mrs. Hitchins showed me how to measure butter and sugar and mix them up in this big machine she had. Mr. Hitchins told silly jokes. And Louella and I talked a lot and laughed at Roxie. It was just nice there.

Was Momma saying I couldn't go?

"I'll bring home cookies for Ruth Ann and Jackson," I said quickly. "We're making peanut butter ones today."

Momma didn't answer. She just looked at me with her frowny face. But then she went to start the car, so I guessed I was going.

Today, Louella and I were finishing our pictures of Roxie. They were a present for her mother's birthday next week. We'd colored them in, and now we were making frames.

Louella met me at the door.

"Quick, come to my room before my momma asks what we're doing!"

We cut out cardboard frames, then sprinkled on some glitter stuff, and we were done. Louella propped up the pictures on her easel.

"Yours is so much better than mine," she said.

"No it isn't," I told her. Well, that was a lie. Her Roxie looked like a curly cloud. But I didn't want to hurt her feelings, so maybe it was an okay lie.

All of a sudden she looked about to cry

"I'm never going to be an artist!" she burst out. "I might as well give up."

"You just need—" I started to say, but she interrupted.

"No, it's true," she said. "I try and try, but nothing comes out right. And my daddy's so set on me being an artist like my gramma. He's going to be real disappointed."

"I don't think so," I said. He was always telling her nice things about everything she did.

Louella wrinkled her nose.

"He doesn't say anything, but I know he cares.

That's the thing about being an only. Your momma and daddy want you to be special. They're always fussing. Like 'Are you sure you're warm enough?' 'Do you need help with your homework?' I know they want me to be happy, but they're on top of me all the time. Sometimes I feel like I can't breathe."

Momma never fussed at me. She left me alone except when she was mad at me.

"My daddy's the worst. When I took ballet, he went out and bought me all kinds of ballet stuff. Like a ballet-dancer doll and Halloween costume and books about famous dancers. I hated it so much, though, he finally had to give up."

She didn't know how lucky she was. If I had a daddy who bought me ballet stuff, I'd be practicing all day.

Louella stopped talking. She looked at me funny, like she didn't know if she should say what she was going to say.

"Weezie," she said, "do you remember your daddy at all?"

I shook my head.

"Did he die before you were born? Or when you were a little baby? If you don't want to talk about it, that's okay."

"Uh, I don't mind," I said. "He went away before

I was born. I don't know where he is or anything. My momma won't tell me."

"Really? Well, that's awful. Why won't she?"

"She hates him. Because he ran out on her, I think. He might be a truck driver, but I can't find out anything else. Well, I do have a picture. And I know his first name."

"You do?" Louella sat up straight. "What is it?"

"Wade," I said. "It was written on the back of the picture along with something else. 'Smoke.' But I don't know what that means."

"Wade. I love that name? Can I see the picture?"

I hesitated. I hadn't planned to show it to anyone. It seemed sort of private. But Louella was my friend. And now she knew about it anyway.

"Sure," I said. "My momma doesn't know I have it. She'd be mad if she did, so I've got it hidden. But I can bring it the next time I come over."

"Oh, do! It's a mystery. Maybe we can solve it. We could find him and then you'll have a daddy."

Louella was bouncing on the bed, she was so excited. I was going to tell her about Calvin and me doing our investigation, but just then her momma knocked on the door.

"I'm ready to start the cookies. Do you girls want to help?"

Mrs. Hitchins had all the baking stuff out on the counter.

"Would it be okay if I make some for my little sister and brother?" I asked.

"Of course."

Mrs. Hitchins was so happy all the time. She had a little sign over the sink that said, "Turn Rain Into Rainbows."

I made heart shapes for Ruth Ann and a truck that turned into a blob after it was baked for Jackson. Mrs. Hitchins wrapped them up pretty in a flower napkin.

"I hope they'll like them, Weezie."

"Oh, they will. Thank you!"

Louella walked me to the door.

"I just had the best idea," she said. "You know how we're going to find your daddy? Well, next Saturday you can sleep over and we'll come up with a plan. What do you think? We can stay up all night. It'll be so much fun!"

It would be fun. And Louella would have good ideas for finding my daddy, I bet. I'd kind of run out of them.

The only problem was Momma. She wouldn't want me sleeping over, I knew.

Well, I'd just have to convince her, that's all.

The Sleepover

I got to sleep over at Louella's house by telling one of my biggest lies yet.

"Her momma's birthday is on Sunday," I told Momma. *(Not true. She'd already had it on Wednesday.)* And Louella's going to surprise her with a special present, but she needs me to help make it. *(Kind of true. The Roxie pictures were a special present, and I'd helped make them.)* And she wants to make a birthday cake too, but she can't do it by herself and her daddy doesn't know how to cook. He's going to blow up all the balloons. Like a hundred. *(I don't know where I got the balloon thing. It just came out.)* So you see, I have to help her."

I looked at Momma with sad eyes, like Ruth Ann did when she was begging for a Tootsie Pop. It always worked for her.

But not for me.

"You want to help her, but not your own momma?" she answered. "Who do you think's going to take care of Ruth Ann and Jackson while I'm at work from five to eleven?"

I'd already thought of that.

"Mrs. Holcomb," I said. "She told me the other day she's happy to help out anytime because she knows you have your hands full."

Well, that was another lie. What she really said was those two were a handful. But when I told her I was invited to sleep over at my friend's house, she said she'd do it because I was such a nice girl.

Momma still didn't want me to go, I could tell, but she couldn't think of another reason to say no. So finally she said, "Just this once, you hear?"

"Yes, Momma."

So I packed my only pajamas without holes and my daddy's picture, and Momma dropped me off at Louella's house.

"Did you bring it?" she asked first thing.

We sat on her tall bed and I pulled out the picture.

"Oh," she said. "He's real handsome! You know

who he looks like? One of the Curtis Brothers in that singing group. Kyle, I think. Yes, Kyle."

It seemed strange to think of my daddy like that.

"Hey, maybe he's a singer!" she said. "He changed his name and got into a singing group. That would be amazing."

"Well, he doesn't look like that now," I reminded her. "He's older."

"I was just kidding. I guess that's his truck next to him. Is that why you think he's a trucker?"

I told her what Gramma Emmeline had said and Uncle Billy Bruner and how Calvin and I'd gone out to the truck stop and Pinkerton Motors.

"Maybe he's not a trucker," I said. "He could be anything. He might even be in jail. That's what Momma told me."

Louella's eyebrows went up.

"But she might've just said that because she hates him."

"Okay," said Louella taking out a notebook. "We have to look for clues."

She stared at the picture, then turned it over.

"Hmmm. I don't see any clues except his name. And 'Smoke.' That could be the name of his truck. You know, it was so old, it smoked. You really don't know what town he was from?"

"No."

"That's what we need to find out. It must be near here, or how would your momma even know him?"

That made sense. I knew Louella would have good ideas.

But before we could work on it, Mrs. Hitchins called us for supper. It was yummy barbequed ribs Mr. Hitchins had made. So I'd told Momma another lie and didn't even know it. Mrs. Hitchins had her Roxie pictures up on the refrigerator. And we had leftover birthday cake. Chocolate. From the bakery.

After supper, Louella spread out her daddy's Oklahoma road map and we looked at the towns nearby. At least six seemed close enough.

Louella wrote them down in her notebook. "Now we just have to follow our clues."

How exactly were we going to do that?

"Calvin can't ride me to all those towns on his bike," I said.

"No. And we don't know his last name so we can't look in the phone book."

We were both quiet, thinking.

"Hey!" said Louella. "We could call Station WSSP and say he's a missing person and they'd put his picture on TV and someone might see it and call in."

That sounded good, except for one thing.

"The police would have to do it," I said. "WSSP wouldn't believe two kids." I knew that from TV.

"I guess so. Okay, here's what we do. We get the picture blown up and put on a giant balloon and we fly it over all those towns."

She must be kidding. Yes, she was smiling.

"Or how about this?" I said. "We get R-o-x-i-e the tracker dog to smell his picture and go find him."

That got us laughing, which made Roxie go bananas, so we played with her for a while. Then we made popcorn and watched part of a movie until Mrs. Hitchins said it was time for bed. I thought we'd stay up all night, but before I knew it I was asleep on the blow-up bed next to Louella's.

In the morning, Mr. Hitchins made pancakes. He really was a good cook. And he pretended to talk French, which made me laugh.

"Time for church," said Mrs. Hitchins. "Weezie, we can drop you off on our way. Unless you'd like to come with us."

I hadn't been to church since Gramma Emmeline used to take me. I was so little my feet stuck straight out on the hard bench and all I could see looking up was the stain-glass windows. The blue in that glass was like slivers of sky.

Momma might not like me going to church. But I didn't want to go home yet. I wanted to pretend that Louella and I were sisters and this was my family.

"Okay," I said.

We drove to a small church outside of town. It didn't look like a church, just a low brown building with regular windows, not stain-glass.

Inside, people surrounded us.

"It's so good to see you! Isn't this the most glorious day? This must be Louella's friend. Hi, honey!"

A tall man with red hair slapped Mr. Hitchins on the back and kissed Mrs. Hitchins' cheek. He had the bluest eyes I ever saw.

"That's Pastor Honeyacre," Louella whispered to me.

"I'm so happy to meet you," he said, folding my hand inside his big, warm one. "Welcome to the Church of the Revelation."

A piano played and everyone sang. Mrs. Hitchins had the happiest smile on her face, which made me want to sing too, so I did. Then came announcements like at school, and people called out names of sick folks who needed God's help, and there were prayers.

Finally Pastor Honeyacre stood up and started talking.

"I want to tell you about the miracle of God's love!" His voice boomed out so loud, you'd think people would hear it all the way in town. "None of your problems are too great for Him! He holds you in the palm of his hand."

Pastor Honeyacre looked so big standing there, it seemed like he could solve everyone's problems himself. He went on a long time, arms waving, blue eyes burning. I didn't understand it all, but then he read a poem about footprints in the sand and the Lord carrying someone in trouble. For some reason, it made me want to cry.

Then the service was over. People smiled and hugged and asked if we were staying for coffee hour.

"Not today," said Mrs. Hitchins. "We have to take Louella's friend home."

We drove to Happy Days without talking much. I was tired from all the singing and praying, and I was still thinking about that poem.

"Well, isn't this nice!" said Mrs. Hitchins.

She couldn't really mean it. The trailer's gray paint was peeling off and the front steps were all crooked.

Momma came out and there was more smiling and shaking hands. Only it didn't feel quite the same as in church.

"We were so glad to have Weezie with us!" said Mrs. Hitchins.

"Well, I hope she wasn't any trouble," Momma said.

I noticed her roots were showing. She needed to get them done again by Marcella. And her t-shirt had a spaghetti-sauce stain down the front.

"Not a bit," said Mrs. Hitchins. "She's so talented. She gave me a wonderful picture of our dog Roxie for my birthday."

"Oh yes," said Momma. "Happy Birthday. How did the cake turn out?"

Uh-oh. The cake we didn't bake.

"It was great!" I said quickly. "Chocolate. Ruth Ann would have loved it, maybe even more than Tootsie Pops."

"I love Tootsie Pops!" Ruth Ann piped up. "Want to see my new Barbie doll? She's got a silver dress and shoes."

Thank goodness for Ruth Ann. That stopped the birthday talk.

"Well, we better be getting home," said Mr. Hitchins.

"Oh," said Mrs. Hitchins. "I hope you don't mind that we took Weezie with us to church this morning. She said it was okay."

"Church?"

"Yes. We go to the Church of the Revelation out on Route 124."

Momma's mouth was smiling, but her eyes weren't. They looked hard at me.

"That's perfectly all right," she said. "Thanks for having her visit."

"Yes, I had a good time," I added.

"We loved having you, Weezie," said Mrs. Hitchins. "Come again."

Looking at Momma, I had the sinking feeling that wasn't going to happen any time soon.

Looking for Clues

"Just tell me, Weezie," said Momma, "why you thought it was okay to go to church with those people. And without even asking me either."

Momma's voice was quiet, but it would get louder. Maybe if I said I was sorry, it wouldn't.

"I'm sorry, Momma," I said. "I should have asked you."

"Yes, you should. What makes you think I'd let you go to church, anyway?"

"I don't know, Momma."

She stopped, like she was remembering something.

"My momma used to take me to church when I

was your age," she said. "And I'd look up at those pretty stained-glass windows and I'd think someone up there was going to take care of me."

Momma had done the same thing I had with Gramma Emmeline. And she liked the windows just like I did. That was kind of nice.

"But I grew up," she went on, "and got smarter. Those preachers make you feel like they care about you, but they don't. All they care about is what you put in the collection basket. And then you go home to your real life and it's just the same old pack of troubles you had before. Nothing they say makes one bit of difference."

That wasn't fair. Pastor Honeyacre really did seem to care. I remembered his big, warm hands wrapped around mine.

"But Momma," I said. "Pastor Honeyacre was real nice. And I didn't put any money in the collection basket."

"Hah! This time you didn't. But you would if you went back there. It's time you learned something, Weezie. No one in this world's going to help you but yourself."

That didn't seem right. Hadn't Louella helped me? And her momma and daddy? And Calvin? And Mrs. Holcomb?

All of a sudden I felt sorry for Momma. I didn't exactly know how to say it, but I had to try.

"You could give your troubles to the Lord," I said. "Pastor Honeyacre says He will help you."

Momma's face turned bright red.

"That's it!" she said. "You're never going back to that church. Not ever. And maybe you shouldn't be spending so much time with that Louella either. Who do those people think they are? Taking you to church without asking! Putting crazy ideas into your head."

I didn't think they were so crazy. But I wasn't going to say it. I'd said too much already. It looked like I wouldn't be going to Louella's house on Saturday. Or sleeping over ever again.

Sure enough, on Saturday I was back in prison on the front step.

I'd told Louella I couldn't come over because I had to take care of Ruth Ann and Jackson. I didn't want her to know Momma was all mad about the church thing.

"Oh." Louella sounded disappointed. "I thought we could work some more on finding your daddy."

"I know. But Momma has to work an extra shift today."

That was another lie. I couldn't keep track of all the lies I'd told. And what if Louella and her momma and daddy decided to go to Pancake Heaven for breakfast and Momma wasn't there? Or saw her with Ruth Ann and Jackson in town? It gave me a stomachache just thinking about it.

If she knew about all my lies, Louella wouldn't want to be my friend anymore. That would be the worst thing.

Now, sitting on the step, I wished Marmalade would come by so I could talk to him. But it was starting to rain. Most likely he wouldn't be around today. So I went inside, climbed up on my bunk, and opened my library book.

I'd taken it out because it was about a boy who ran away like I wanted to when Momma yelled at me. This boy ran away from his apartment in the city to live in a tree. That was amazing. He was so brave and smart. I didn't know if I could live in a tree, though. What if it rained for days and days and you couldn't go out? What if you had to go to the bathroom in the middle of the night? Maybe a tent would be better. Or some kind of shack.

That made me think of my daddy. If only I could find him, I could run away to his house.

Suddenly I dropped my book. Why did I have to

go to Louella's house to work on finding him? I could look for clues right here in the trailer. I'd found the photograph. Maybe I'd find something else.

I jumped down and went to Momma's room. You could hardly walk in there, it was so crowded. She had the whole bedroom set from Gramma Emmeline's old house: bed, a tall dresser and a short one, and a dressing table with a big mirror. It was too much for the trailer. Momma knew it.

"But all that stuff was my momma's," she said once when I asked her. "I couldn't sell it."

I started with the dressers. Mostly they just had clothes. Except for a bottom drawer. It was stuffed with papers. I started taking them out. Bills—nothing but bills. Gas, electric, the bank. Some had "Second Notice" on the envelope. Did that mean Momma hadn't paid them?

This wasn't what I was looking for. I put them back and tried the dressing table. Nothing. The only place left was the closet.

It was as crammed as every place else. I moved boots and a broken umbrella. Then I saw a cardboard box. I dragged it out. More papers. Not bills this time, just a jumble of things Momma had saved for some reason.

Oh, I bet I'd find a clue in here! I pulled out some

old photos of us when we were babies. Ruth Ann was the cutest, I had to admit, with her wispy blond hair, always smiling. I looked kind of worried, and Jackson had a fat face and no hair. A few were of Momma and Tommy. They seemed really young, and happy. I couldn't remember when Momma looked like that. No pictures of Roy, and no more of my daddy.

That was disappointing. I took out more stuff: magazine clippings about hair styles, an ad for a beauty school in Tulsa, Ruth Ann's picture of a tree with apples. And a pencil drawing of a little square house with writing that said "Our House. Love, Tommy." That made me sad. Why did he have to go off and get killed?

There were clippings from newspapers too, mostly about beauty pageants. I guessed Momma was serious about entering Ruth Ann. And one showing someone dressed up like a bee.

It must be Momma, dressed for Halloween. Only it didn't look like a kid's costume. It was more like a grown-up one. Next to the bee were a couple of girls. I couldn't make them out, the paper was so old and creased. And the place below the picture, just where the printing would be, had been torn out.

This didn't seem like a clue. But I hadn't found anything else, so I left it out. At the bottom of the box were a few baby things, a lopsided clay bowl I'd made in kindergarten *(Momma saved that?)*, a stick with twisted yellow ribbons attached to it *(what was that?)*, and another old photo. This one was of Gramma Emmeline with me on her lap. Gramma looked like she used to before she got sick, and we both had great big smiles on our faces. I'd never seen that picture before. I needed to have it.

I glanced over at Momma's alarm clock. She could be home any time now. Quick, I stuffed everything back in the box except the Gramma photo and the newspaper clipping and shoved the box back in the closet.

I was about to get out of there when I saw something I hadn't noticed before. On Momma's dressing table, next to Tommy's picture, was a bit of chipped china with a rose on it. The lid from Gramma Emmeline's teapot.

That was a surprise. Momma hadn't really thrown it all away. She'd kept a little piece of it.

Just like I had.

Capturing
Marmalade

I kept the photograph of Gramma Emmeline with the one of my daddy, and I looked at it every night. It made me feel like she was still with me in some kind of way. And I took the newspaper clipping to school.

I showed it to Louella at lunchtime.

"Is it a clue, do you think?" I asked.

"It looks like a Halloween costume. But not a little kid one, like you said." Louella shook her head. "Maybe it's not your momma. Maybe it's somebody else."

"Maybe. But then why would she save it?"

We both stared at the photo for a while. Too bad

the caption underneath was missing. All I could make out were the first two letters: "Pe." The rest was torn away.

"You know what?" I said. "It's probably not a clue at all, just a picture of her at Halloween. And she saved it because it was in the newspaper."

"I guess so," said Louella.

I stuck the clipping back in my book bag, and we got in line for lunch.

That afternoon was warm and sunny, so I figured I'd do my homework outside. I started on my math worksheet. I liked to do that first because it was the hardest.

"Rourr."

I looked up and there was Marmalade. Sitting where he always sat, tail curled around his paws, on Mrs. Holcomb's step. Looking like he knew a lot even if he never said anything.

He seemed glad to listen. I guessed he was getting used to me, because he didn't move one bit when I talked to him.

I told him about how Louella was helping me find my daddy, and how we had a great sleepover at her house with her dog, Roxie.

"You probably wouldn't like Roxie," I said. "She's

kind of hyper. But then I messed up about church and Momma got mad and now I'm in prison again. And if Louella finds out about my lies, she's going to hate me."

Marmalade didn't even fall asleep while I was talking. He kept looking at me with his green eyes. As if he understood.

"You know what else?" I whispered. "I kind of wish I could live at Louella's house. It's really nice there, and her momma never yells. Is that a bad thing to wish?"

I'd never said it out loud before. But Marmalade didn't even blink. So I kept going.

"Momma's always mad at me, no matter what I do. She never gets mad at Ruth Ann or Jackson. Just me."

I felt sad saying that. Of course Marmalade didn't answer, but I thought he looked sad too. If only he'd come closer. I wanted him to curl up next to me so I could pat him, like the man with the bear cub.

That gave me an idea.

"Don't go away," I told him.

I went inside and opened a can of tuna and brought it outside. But this time I didn't put the can in the weeds. I set it down next to me on the step.

"Look what I have for you," I said.

Marmalade sat up straight. His ears pricked up.

"Doesn't it smell good? It's tuna. Come and have some."

He was thinking about it, I could tell. He walked in a circle around the flower pots, then sat down again.

"It's okay," I said in my softest voice. "I'm not going to hurt you. We're friends."

Marmalade's tail swished back and forth, but he stayed on the step.

I held out the tuna can.

"Come on," I whispered. "You can do it."

Marmalade sat on his step, looking at me. I sat on mine, looking at him. Why wouldn't he jump down and come over? I needed him to do that.

Maybe if I brought the tuna closer. I stood up, stretching out my hand.

Marmalade jumped. In a flash of yellow, he was off the step, landing soft as one of those big cats in the wild. And then he was gone in the tall grass. I watched him stalk away, his head and tail held high.

The air went out of me like a leaky balloon. I'd moved too fast and scared him. I hadn't been patient, like the man with the bear cub. Now he might never come back. Why did I have to mess everything up?

I sat there for a while looking down at the dirt. Inside my head, I still saw the way Marmalade looked when he stalked away from me. It was the look I'd seen so many times before. Proud, like a king. Like he owned the world, even though he was only a dirty stray cat.

I had to draw that feeling. Quick, I opened my notebook. He'd disappeared now, but the picture was frozen in my brain, like something drawn on the blackboard at school. I had to work fast before that picture faded away.

It didn't, though. I was amazed. It felt like the lines were flowing from inside my head to my fingers and out through my pencil. I drew his straight-up tail, the curves of his legs, the round face and tri-angle ears. It was the way the shapes fit together, I saw, that made the difference. That gave me the feeling I wanted.

I drew a few lines of grass and I was finished. All of a sudden I felt worn out. I closed my eyes. Had I done it? Had I captured that cat?

Opening my eyes, I looked down at my picture. It was rough, just a sketch. It needed to be filled in and colored. But I felt a little tingle of excitement.

I'd done it. I'd got Marmalade.

The Art Show

"Oh!" said Ms. Martinelli.

That was all. What did it mean? Did she like my Marmalade picture or not?

She stared at it for another long minute.

Then she said, "You've done it, Weezie. You've said something about that cat. It has a high opinion of itself, doesn't it?"

"Yes," I said.

She liked it! And she saw what I was trying to draw. Not only did she like it, she wanted me to turn it into a painting.

"It will be even more powerful with strong colors," she said.

So I worked on it the next three art periods, using real art paper and paints. Bright blue for the sky, green grass, and orangey-yellow cat. And it came out just like she said.

"Yes!" said Ms. Martinelli, as if I'd just scored a goal or something.

"It looks like it's walking right off the paper," said Louella.

Even the boys liked it.

"Watch out!" said Farley Wilcox. "That tiger might bite."

After class, Ms. Martinelli called me up front.

"I'd like to include your painting in the art show," she said. "You know, the one we're having for Parents' Night. Is that okay, Weezie?"

Okay? It was more than okay. Ms. Martinelli had started the art show this year. She picked the best artwork of the whole school for the whole year and put it up in the front hall where the parents would see it first thing.

"Sure," I said, my mouth breaking into a big smile.

"That's so great!" said Louella as we left the art room.

I couldn't stop smiling. Ms. Martinelli had picked my picture! It was going to be up in the front hall where everyone would see it. I felt like turning cart-wheels, which I didn't really know how to do.

"Oh, I bet your momma will be so happy!"

I wasn't so sure about that. "Maybe," I said.

"She will! I know my daddy'd be over the moon. Ms. Martinelli only picks two or three from each grade, so you know yours is extra-special."

That was true. Nothing of mine had ever been extra-special before.

I told Momma the minute she got home from work.

"That's nice," she said. "It smells like Jackson's got a mess in his diaper. Why didn't you change him?"

"I will," I said. "Momma, this is special. Ms. Martinelli only picks a couple from each grade and she picked mine. My picture's going to be up in the front hall for Parents' Night. You have to come see it."

"When's that?"

"Next Wednesday. Seven o'clock."

"Okay, I'll try and make it. Unless Frankie makes me work an extra shift."

"Mrs. Holcomb can babysit. You know she likes to help out."

"Okay, Weezie, okay. Now will you change Jackson's diaper?"

"Yes, Momma."

Ms. Martinelli sure was serious about the art show. She got Mr. Tatum, the custodian, to drape the hall with black cloth and put up shelves. It was going to look like a real art museum, like the one she took us to in Tulsa last fall.

We rode in the school bus, past those oil pumper things that everyone said made Oklahoma what it is today, and suddenly we were in the city. I never saw so many tall buildings. Or so many paintings as in that museum. Ms. Martinelli said each one told a story. I didn't understand what she meant then but I did now.

Louella and I looked at my picture, propped up on the work table with the other fifth-grade art show projects.

"Yours is definitely the best," said Louella. "Jimmy Hollins' robot is weird. And Tammy's pot is okay, but it's just a pot."

Louella was the one who wanted to be an artist, but she didn't seem to mind that it was me who was picked for the show. She really was a good friend.

"You need to print a name for your painting on this card," said Ms. Martinelli.

Real artists in the museum in Tulsa had crazy names for their work, like "Rainy June Moon" or "Study #37." I could call my painting "King of the

World." Or maybe "Marmalade." But that sounded like jam. Or I could call it what it was.

"Stray Cat," I printed on the card. And my name, "Grace Louise Dawson." My artist name. That felt good.

"Could you girls help set up the show after school tomorrow?" Ms. Martinelli asked. "I know I'll need help."

"Sure," said Louella.

"I think so," I said. I really wanted to do it, but I'd have to ask Momma.

Just as I expected, she wasn't happy about it.

"Who's going to take care of Ruth Ann and Jackson?" she asked. "I said I'd come to your show. Isn't that enough? Really, Weezie, you don't think of anyone but yourself."

"Mrs. Holcomb will do it," I said. "She'll just come early."

"Then you better ask her."

Mrs. Holcomb agreed, as always. "Of course I'll help out. This is a big night for you, isn't it, Weezie?"

It was fun setting up the art show with Ms. Martinelli. Louella and I carried all the art to the front hall and Ms. Martinelli told us where to put each piece.

"That clay dinosaur, over there. No, wait! Maybe next to the owl."

141

She kept changing her mind. But finally she stood back and looked. "Yes," she said. "What do you girls think?"

It was amazing. The hall we walked in and out of every day had turned into an art museum.

"It's perfect," I said.

Louella and I sat on the floor, nibbling on the corn chips and banana her momma had packed for her.

"I think yours is the best of the whole show," she said. "Too bad Ms. Martinelli doesn't give out prizes. You'd win for sure."

"What about that sixth-grader, Lloyd Danner?"

He'd done a painting of a man with a long face and big nose. He said it was his grampa, but some kids thought it was Mr. McCracken, the principal.

"His is good, but I like yours better."

We went to the girls' room to wash our hands. Ms. Martinelli was there, trying to calm her wild hair. She'd changed into her brightest outfit yet, an orange blouse and long, turquoise, flowery skirt.

"You two have been such a help," she said. "Would you like to stand by the door and greet the parents when they come in? Make sure they look at the art show before going to the classrooms."

This was good. I'd be right there when Momma came.

142

"And tell your momma to visit the art room, Weezie. I want to talk to her about your work. And about the art class I'll be giving this summer. I hope you'll be able to come to it."

An art class this summer? Oh, I'd really like that!

At seven, we were waiting by the front door. Mr. and Mrs. Hitchins were the first to arrive.

"That one must be yours," said Mrs. Hitchins right away. "Oh, Weezie, it's wonderful!"

Mr. Hitchins shook my hand about twenty-five times. "Congratulations!"

A bunch of parents I didn't know came in, then Calvin with his grandmother. He stared at my picture for the longest time.

"I know that cat," he said finally. "Once I gave it a potato chip. But it didn't like it."

"He likes tuna fish," I said watching the door.

Where was Momma? Maybe Ruth Ann was having one of her tantrums and she had to calm her down.

"Hi, Weezie!"

Wouldn't you know, it was Ruby with her five skinny brothers and her daddy. He was wearing clean jeans and a white collar shirt. I'd never seen him dressed up like that before.

"This is my daddy," she said with her best smirk, grabbing his hand.

She was the wormiest worm I ever met.

"I know," I said, hoping he didn't remember me from the hardware store.

"Come on, Daddy!" said Ruby. "I'll show you my classroom." And she went prancing down the hall.

"She didn't even look at the art show," said Louella.

"Who cares?" I said.

People kept arriving, only none of them was Momma. Maybe her car wouldn't start. She kept saying the battery was about to quit.

But she'd promised she'd be there. She was just late, that's all.

Fewer and fewer parents were coming in now. I looked up at the clock. 7:20. Momma was really late.

"Do you think something happened to her?" Louella asked.

"Maybe her car wouldn't start," I said. "Or maybe my little brother got sick. He gets ear infections. But she's coming."

I peered out into the parking lot, wishing hard I'd see Momma's little green car pulling in. But it wasn't there.

Come on, Momma, I thought. *You said you'd come. You can't break a promise.*

Then it was 7:45 and I knew. She wasn't coming.

Louella looked at me. "Something must have happened like you said."

"I bet it was Jackson. He was real crabby this morning. He must have come down with something."

That had to be it.

Mr. and Mrs. Hitchins drove me home, still talking about my picture and what a wonderful teacher Ms. Martinelli was even if some people thought she was strange.

I knew they were trying to make me feel better. But I couldn't get my face to smile or any words to come out of my mouth.

Momma didn't come, I kept thinking. *She never came.*

Vroom!

When I opened the door to the trailer, Momma was sitting in her reclining chair watching TV. No Mrs. Holcomb. No Jackson, crying and holding his ear.

"What happened?" I asked her.

Momma didn't look up from her show, where two skinny blonde girls with hardly any clothes on were talking to a handsome lifeguard.

"Happened? I had to work late, that's all. We got really busy and Juanita came in late, so I couldn't leave."

"But you promised you'd come! To see my picture in the art show."

Momma turned the sound down.

"I'm sorry. But I can't do everything, you know. I work hard every single day, carrying those heavy trays and wiping up sticky syrup and listening to Frankie's gripes. And you want me to come to your school, at night, to see a picture you drew."

"It wasn't—"

"Wasting your time drawing pictures instead of helping out here." Momma's voice rose. "And going to that Louella's fancy house so her momma and daddy can put fancy ideas in your head. That's not where you belong. You have to learn your place, Weezie."

What did that mean?

Before I had a chance to ask, she turned up the TV again.

"I'm tired," she said. "And I want to see the rest of my show. Go to bed, Weezie."

I stared at the TV. Now the blondes were dancing at some club with palm trees. They must be in Florida. Where my daddy and I were going, I used to think. That was such a dumb idea.

"But it was the art show," I mumbled. "It was special."

"Go to bed," Momma said again.

I went. But not to sleep.

I lay listening to Ruth Ann and Jackson breathe and seeing in my head everything that had happened. My picture on the wall and Ms. Martinelli in her pretty outfit and wormy Ruby with her daddy and me waiting by the front door. Waiting and waiting for Momma's car that never came.

Why wouldn't she come after I begged her? And I got Mrs. Holcomb to babysit and everything.

Momma hates me, I thought. *That's why.*

Hate. That was a terrible word. But the minute I thought it, I knew it was true. Everything Momma said and did proved it. I'd known it for a long time, maybe forever. I just didn't want to know it.

I felt empty inside. I squeezed my eyes shut, but tears ran down into my pillow anyway.

My own momma hates me.

In the morning I could hardly drag myself out of bed.

"You're going to miss the bus!" Momma kept yelling.

Finally I got myself up and out the door without looking at her.

On the bus, Calvin said, "That was a good cat you made."

"Thanks," I mumbled, hardly hearing him.

At school, Louella asked, "What happened to your momma last night? Was Jackson real sick?"

I nodded. "But he's better now."

What was wrong with me? Why couldn't I tell her the truth?

Because I'm bad, that's why. And that's the real truth.

At art, Ms. Martinelli said, "Thanks again for your help, Weezie. I'm so sorry your momma couldn't make it to the art show."

"My little brother was sick," I told her. I might as well keep lying. It didn't matter anyway.

When I got home I was so tired out, I didn't feel like doing anything. Not drawing, that was for sure. I sat on the step and stared at the dirt. Ants were running around, busy as could be. One was carrying something bigger than it was. It kept dropping it and picking it up again. I thought it would have to give up, but it didn't. It just kept trying to carry its heavy load.

I was so busy watching the ants, I didn't hear Mrs. Atchley drive up.

"Look what I made!" cried Ruth Ann. "It's a macaroni bracelet."

How could she be so happy when I was so sad? Oh, that's right. Momma loves her.

"Vroom!" said Jackson, pointing down the hill.

Oh no, not Roy again. Not today.

But it was. He coasted to a stop next to me. He looked different. Like something had bucked him up a little.

"Hey, Weezie!" he said. "Guess what?"

I forced myself to answer. "You got a job?"

"Not exactly," said Roy. "But I may be getting into a training program, over in Claremore. They've got a new auto parts factory opening up next year."

"That would be great," I said, trying to sound excited. It really would be.

"Keep your fingers crossed for me. Hey, little buddy!" He swooped Jackson up and set him in front of him on his bike. "This is how you make it go, see? And that's the horn. Beep beep!"

They looked real nice, their two dark heads close together, Roy's arm around Jackson's middle.

"Now let's go for a ride."

What was he thinking? Momma would have a fit if she found out.

"You can't do that!" I said.

"Don't pop a gasket. We're not going any place."

The bike started moving. No motor, just Roy's feet pushing, but still.

"It's okay, Weezie," he said. "I know what I'm doing."

He went in a wide circle, past Mrs. Holcomb's trailer, than back to ours. Jackson loved it. He was laughing and squealing. "Beep, beep!"

That's when Momma's car rode up the hill. She jammed on the brakes and was out the door almost before it stopped.

"What on God's earth do you think you're doing!" she screamed. "Give me my baby!"

She grabbed for Jackson, but Roy held onto him.

"Hey, Charlene, cool it," he said. "I wasn't going to hurt him. You ought to know that."

"Hah! Coming here behind my back, riding him around on that bike of yours. How long has this been going on? Weezie, have you been in on this?

"No, I haven't, Momma," I said.

"You give me my baby right now!" she cried. "And get out of here before I call the police."

She tried to grab Jackson again, but Roy wouldn't let go.

"He's my baby too," he said. "You can't keep him away from me. It isn't right. I'm his daddy."

He seemed so calm and grown up all of a sudden.

Jackson was crying now. Roy handed him to me.

"Come on, Charlene. Let's go inside and talk."

But Momma was having none of that.

"You think you can sweet-talk me into getting your way? You've got no right to him. Have you ever given me one penny to feed this baby? Or taken him to the Walk-In when he was sick? You can't even get a job pumping gas! And what about that little manicurist you're running around with? I know about her."

She was beating on his chest with her fists.

Roy just stood there and let her do it.

"That's not true about Lila," he tried to say, but Momma kept yelling.

"You're no good, Roy Dixon! You're just like the rest of them. Like her daddy!"

She was looking at me now. Suddenly she snatched Jackson out of my arms, grabbed Ruth Ann, and ran inside.

Roy didn't move. He looked like he'd been hit by a truck. I felt pretty much the same. I could hear Ruth Ann and Jackson both bawling.

Momma opened the door again.

"You get on that bike and ride out of here!" she yelled. "Or I'll call the police. Don't think I won't!"

"You do that!" Roy yelled back. "I don't care."

152

He jumped on his motorcycle. The engine roared to life.

I looked at the trailer and back at Roy.

"Wait!" I said. "I'm coming with you."

He reached out a hand and I climbed on behind him. And we went vrooming out of there.

Getaway

This wasn't like riding on Calvin's bike. The motorcycle went so fast, everything whizzed by in a flash—houses, trees, the Pig Stand barbeque place. It was so loud, I couldn't talk. Roy didn't seem to want to talk anyway. His back was stiff where I held onto him, and he didn't turn his head.

We were heading away from town. That was good.

Roy kept going. No houses now, just a blur of blacktop with green trees and red dirt on each side.

I closed my eyes, feeling the wind blowing my hair. It felt so good leaving everything behind. Riding fast down some road. Who cares where it's going? Maybe we'd ride clear down to Texas. Or head east till we came to Florida. Just like my dream, we'd end up at Disney World and I'd have the last laugh on Ruby. Only instead of my daddy, it'd be Roy and me. And for sure we'd swim with the dolphins.

How would their noses feel? Like rubber? Could I climb on their backs and go for a ride?

After a long time, I felt the bike slowing down. Where were we? In the middle of no place, it looked like.

Roy braked to a stop and turned to look at me.

"You okay?"

I nodded.

"Do you want to go back? I can take you."

"No!" I never wanted to go back.

I couldn't see Roy's face inside his helmet, but then he took it off and he was smiling.

"Me neither," he said.

He killed the motor and swung off the bike. All of a sudden it was quiet.

"So this is the place," he said.

I didn't see anything, just scrubby trees and sagging barbwire fence. And way back some kind of falling-down building.

"What place?"

"Where they're going to build the auto-parts factory. Right here outside of Claremore. Isn't that something? There'll be hundreds of new jobs, they say. And I'm going to get one of them."

He looked tickled to pieces, looking at that land with nothing on it.

"Well, that'll be real good," I said.

"And then Charlene will have to listen to me. I'll have money to give her for Jackson. And if she makes a fuss, I'll hire myself a lawyer. She'll see, I mean to be a daddy to that boy."

Roy seemed so hopeful now. It was good to see.

"Hey, Weezie. Want a bite of candy bar?"

He dug in his pocket and came out with a smooshed Snickers bar. He handed me half and sat down in the grass. I sat next to him.

"So what about you, Weezie? Why'd you run off like that?"

My throat felt closed up. I swallowed hard.

"It's Momma," I said. "She hates me."

Roy looked surprised.

"Nah. She's hard all right, but she can't hate you."

"She does," I said. "She thinks I'm bad like my daddy. And she hates him."

"She was just mad, that's all. At me, mostly."

"That's not all." The words poured out in a flood. "She didn't come to my art show at school and she doesn't like me drawing pictures or going to my friend Louella's house. She was real mad when they took me to church. And she thinks I tell lies. Well, I do sometimes. I don't know why. And she won't even tell me who my daddy is!"

Suddenly I was crying in sobs that shook my whole body. I didn't know that would happen.

Roy was looking at me like *uh-oh, what do I do now?*

"Hey," he said. "It's okay."

That made me cry even harder. My head hurt and my nose got all snotty like Jackson's and still I couldn't stop.

Roy didn't say anything. After a while I felt him patting my back. *Pat, pat, pat* like I was a little baby. I took some deep breaths, and it was over. I felt hollow, like the tears had drained out my insides.

"I'm sorry," I said.

"It's okay," said Roy. "Good to get it out."

He leaned back, looking at the sky. Its color was fading as the sun went down behind the trees.

"You know, your momma's had a lot of troubles in her life," he said. "Losing Tommy like that, and your gramma too. And having to work for Frankie at the pancake place instead of opening a beauty shop like she wanted."

I guessed that was true. But it wasn't my fault.

"So what are you going to do, Weezie?" he asked.

"I'm not going back," I said. "Can't we keep going? We could go to Florida. Maybe Disney World. I always wanted to go there. Didn't you?"

"I did when I was a little kid," said Roy. "Then what would we do?"

"I don't know. You could get a job and I could go to school."

I could see us there, in a little pink house with palm trees. *And you could be my daddy,* I thought, but I didn't say it. I didn't say the part about swimming with the dolphins either.

"That sounds pretty good," said Roy.

It did? I was kind of surprised he agreed.

"Only it wouldn't work. Your momma would have the police chasing after me in a minute. Anyway, I can't go anyplace now. I need to stay here and get my training and start that job so I can see Jackson."

"Oh. I guess so." That made sense for him, but not for me.

Roy chewed on the end of a long blade of grass.

"It's hard," he said. "Standing up to your momma, I mean. She can be pretty scary. I stayed clear of her for a long time, but now I've made up my mind to do it. Maybe you should too."

No, I said inside my head. *Don't you understand? She hates me.*

I looked over at the motorcycle. If only I could jump on and keep riding to a place where no one would ever find me. But where? Florida was so far off and I had no money and it would be dark soon. Besides, I didn't even know how to start the engine.

"Come on, Weezie," said Roy. "I'll buy you a burger and then we'll head back and talk to your momma."

I guessed we had to. "Okay," I said.

We rode into Claremore. A McDonald's was right ahead and across from it a Wendy's. But Roy turned in at the Getty station.

"Just want to talk to Earl here about that training program," he said. "Make sure my name's on the list. It'll only take a minute."

I saw him talking to a big man in a cowboy hat. They were laughing. It was good to see Roy laugh for a change.

"It's all set," he said when he came back. "So which will it be, McDonald's or Wendy's?"

Before I could answer, a black and white car with one of those flasher things pulled in front, blocking our way. A man got out and walked toward us.

"Oh no," Roy muttered. "She went and did it."

Did what? I thought. Then I realized. Momma had called the police.

The policeman was young, with blond hair and a red face.

"Are you Roy Dixon?" he asked.

"Yes, sir," said Roy.

"And this is Grace Louise Dawson?"

"Yes, sir," I said.

"I just took her for a ride on my bike," said Roy. "That's all."

"And we were going to have a burger and then go home," I added.

"That's all that's happening here," said Roy.

But the policeman shook his head.

"We were told there had been a kidnapping. Man on a motorcycle rode off with a young girl."

A kidnapping? Why would Momma say that?

"I'm going to have to take you to the station," the policeman said. "You won't be giving me any trouble now, will you?"

"No, sir," said Roy.

It was just like on TV. He took us both by our arms and led us to his police car and put us in the back seat. Ducking our heads so they wouldn't bump.

I couldn't believe this was happening. Roy was getting arrested and maybe me too.

And we hadn't even run off to Florida.

The Truth

That same policeman drove me home. He even bought me a burger at Wendy's, and I ate it in the car. But Roy had to stay at the station. They were keeping him in jail overnight.

"That's not fair," I told the policeman. "He didn't do anything."

"Your momma thinks he did," he said. "She'll have to come to the station and decide if she wants to press charges."

"But it was me that wanted to go for a ride, not Roy."

"Then he'll be okay. You just tell your momma that, and likely everything will work out."

Officer Dwayne Hicks, his name was. I'd never met a policeman before and he was nice, I have to say. Not like some of the ones on TV. He never took out his gun, not one time.

He rode me back home in the dark. I thought how a few hours ago I was riding the other way, wanting never to go back, and here I was riding home in a police car. What would Momma say? Would she be real mad? Of course she would. I wished Officer Hicks could drive a little slower.

Then we were there. Momma must have been listening for the car because she was at the door right away, standing in the yellow light. She ran toward me, her arms open wide. I thought for a second she was going to hug me. But instead she grabbed me by the shoulders.

"Weezie!" she said. "Are you all right?"

"I'm fine," I said. "I just went for a ride with Roy, that's all."

"A ride?" Now she was shaking me. "That no-good Roy kidnaps you and you call it going for a ride? I know what he was up to, trying to punish me about Jackson! Did he hurt you?"

"Of course not, Momma. He would never do that."

The policeman stepped out of the car.

"I'm Officer Hicks of the Claremore police,

ma'am," he said. "Sounds like we've got two different stories going on here. You'll have to come to the
station in the morning and sort it out. Decide if you
want to press charges."

"I will," said Momma.

"Well then, you better get your daughter to bed.
If everything's all right here, I'll say goodnight."

"Thank you for bringing her home," said Momma.

"Good night!" I called. "And thanks for the burger."

The minute we got inside, Momma said, "Now
you tell me exactly what happened. I want the truth,
no lies."

"I told you," I said. "He just took me for a ride."

Her eyes drilled into mine.

"That's not the whole story. Something happened,
didn't it? Did Roy put his hands on you?"

"No!"

Now was the time to do what Roy said. Stand
up and tell Momma the whole truth. No lies. That's
what she'd asked for.

My chest got so tight, it was difficult to breathe.

"I—" I started, and stopped.

"You what?"

"I wanted to go," I got out. "He didn't make me.
I—I was running away."

Momma looked like she didn't understand.

I stared at the floor, at Ruth Ann's Las Vegas Barbie. Her silver dress was ripped, I noticed.

"Because-you-hate-me," I said in a rush.

Momma stared at me. She took a long breath, blew it out, and sat down in her chair.

"Well, that's not true," she said.

It is, I thought. *It is.*

She pressed her fingers to her forehead the way she did when she was getting one of her headaches.

"You don't know what it's like," she said finally. "Trying to raise up three kids on your own with no one to help. And working day and night at a crappy job with a boss who yells at you all the time about nothing."

Her face was squeezed like she was about to cry, but she didn't.

"And you," she said, "the spitting image of your no-good daddy, reminding me of him every single day. You have to understand, he was bad. Didn't give a hoot in hell about anyone but himself and football and his precious truck. And lies! You couldn't believe a word out of his mouth. I don't care about that blond majorette, he says. We'll get married and move to California, he says. Hah! And one day he just ups and drives away in that truck of his, leaving me with a big bump in my belly that turns out to be you. You may think I'm a little hard on you, a little strict. But I swear I won't let you grow up to be like him!"

So that was it. I already knew, really, but now she'd said it straight out. It was on account of my daddy she hated me.

I couldn't help it. Tears started rolling down my face. I couldn't say anything or I'd be out-and-out bawling like before.

Momma didn't say anything more either, just sat still in her chair.

Then I thought about Roy. He wasn't bad. I had to make sure Momma didn't send him to prison.

"You're not going to press charges, are you? Really, Roy didn't do anything. And he didn't get to tell you, but they're building an auto parts factory in Claremore. He signed up for a training program so pretty soon he'll have a good job and can give you money for Jackson."

"Well, it's about time," said Momma.

"So you won't press charges?" I had to hear her say it.

"Do you swear this running off was all your idea? And you're telling the truth, he didn't touch you? I mean it. You have to tell me the truth."

The truth was he did touch me—*pat, pat, pat* on

the back. Unlike Momma, who couldn't even hug me. It had been a long time since anyone touched me, maybe since Gramma Emmeline, and it had felt good. But that's not what she meant, I knew.

"I swear, Momma."

She looked hard at me, trying to decide whether to believe me or not. I looked right back.

"Then I guess we can forget it."

That was a relief. Now Roy could get out of jail in the morning. I had one more thing I needed to say, though.

"Roy isn't no-good like my daddy," I said. "He really cares about Jackson. He wants to come visit him and take him places and be his daddy."

Momma frowned. "We'll see about that."

Well, I guessed she wasn't about to change her mind just because I said so.

There was something else. Should I say it? I might as well.

"Didn't you ever like Roy?"

Momma sniffed. "Sure I did." Were those tears in her eyes? I couldn't tell. Her voice turned hard again. "But I couldn't count on him. I couldn't count on any of them. Not even Tommy."

All of a sudden I felt so tired I couldn't stand up.

My eyes were falling out of my head and I had no words left.

Momma looked wrung out too.

"I've got to get to bed," she said, "so I can go over to that police station early. Frankie'll be all in a twist if I'm late for work."

I dragged myself to the bathroom to brush my teeth. Looking in the mirror, I saw ketchup on my nose and grass stuck in my hair. I pulled out a long piece and chewed on the end like Roy had.

"I spoke up about you," I said to the mirror.

It looked like I'd saved him from jail. That made me feel good.

And bad too. Bad that my daddy wasn't like Roy. He'd run out on Momma, but not just her. Me too. His own little baby. Hadn't he ever wondered how I was doing? Hadn't he ever wanted to come back and see?

I scrubbed my face so hard it hurt and then crawled off to bed.

A Bee with Big Feet

Everything seemed strange.

Roy was out of jail. I knew that. But he didn't come over to see Jackson or talk to Momma or me.

Momma and I weren't talking to each other either. Sometimes I saw her looking at me in kind of a different way. But after that night, it seemed like there was nothing left to say.

And Louella kept asking me stuff, like why couldn't I come to her house on Saturday and was something wrong, and I didn't know what to say. I wasn't going to tell her any more lies.

"Is it your momma?" she asked finally.

I felt those stupid tears sneaking up on me again. I just nodded.

"I thought so," said Louella. "I know she's pretty strict. And she needs you to take care of your little sister and brother. They're so cute! But we can still eat lunch together."

Why was she so nice? I didn't deserve a friend like Louella.

She hadn't forgotten about finding my daddy either.

"Do you still have that newspaper picture of your momma dressed like a bee?" she asked the next day at lunch.

"Yes." It was in my backpack.

"Let's look at it again at recess."

"Okay."

So we went to the farthest corner of the playground, away from the boys' kickball game and the girls whispering by the swings. I smoothed out the newspaper picture in the grass.

"So why did you want to look at it again?" I asked.

Louella took a little round magnifying glass out of her pocket.

"I don't know. I just thought something about that Halloween costume wasn't right. Maybe if we look closer, we might see something."

She peered through the glass.

"That's it!" she said suddenly.

"What?"

"Does your momma have big feet?"

"No. Mine are almost as big as hers."

"Look at the feet," she said, handing me the glass.

Louella was right. This bee was wearing really big sneakers.

"Those are boys' feet," I said.

Boy, bee. No, not a bee. Something clicked inside my head.

"It's a Yellowjacket," I said.

That's what our high school football team calls itself.

"Yes!" said Louella. "That has to be the team mascot. And those girls must be cheerleaders."

I'd hardly noticed the girls. I looked again. Magnified, I saw long, dark hair, short skirts, light-colored sweaters, and something in their hands.

All of a sudden I knew.

"That's Momma!" I said. "The one on the left. And the other one is her friend, Marcella."

It made sense now. I'd seen a couple of old yellow sweaters in Momma's drawers. And that stick with yellow ribbons I'd found in the box was what they had in their hands. Some kind of pompom thing.

"Whatcha doing?"

I looked up at Ruby's skinny legs in the Mickey Mouse shorts she'd been wearing since it turned warm.

"Nothing you'd be interested in," Louella said right off.

"Lemme see!" said Ruby.

I grabbed the newspaper picture and turned it upside down.

"I told you, it's none of your business!" said Louella.

"Yeah," I said, giving Ruby my worst glare. "So leave us alone."

She looked down at the newspaper and up at us, like she couldn't decide what to do.

"Oh, have your dumb old secrets!" she said finally. "See if I care."

And she flounced off to bother someone else.

I turned over the newspaper, staring at Momma's picture. She never told me she was a cheerleader, or whatever those pompom girls were called.

"This could be a clue," said Louella. "We know your daddy came from a different town. So maybe a football game was how they met."

That sounded right. Football was a big thing in our town. Lots of people traveled around to go to games.

Now what?

"If we could look at some more old newspapers," I said slowly, "we could see what teams the Yellowjackets played. Then we'd know the towns he might have come from."

Louella's face lit up. "I know where they keep old newspapers," she said. "In the library. My daddy went there once to look something up."

"Then that's where we need to go."

"When can we do it? Maybe Saturday?"

I already knew what Momma was doing Saturday. Taking Ruth Ann and Jackson to the discount store to shop for sneakers on sale. I could get Calvin to ride me to the library. He'd like to go on another investigation.

"I'll see you there," I said. "Ten o'clock?"

"Ten o'clock."

Emergency!

After school I was walking up the hill, still thinking about the girl in the newspaper picture. It was hard to believe Momma could ever have been that girl. Jumping up and down, waving those pompom things. It just didn't seem like her. But it was.

As I got close to the trailer, I saw something lying by the front step. Ruth Ann's sweater, it looked like. She must have dropped it.

Wait. That wasn't a sweater. That was Marmalade lying there!

But something was wrong. Coming closer, I saw blood. His face and back and tail were covered with it. And one of his back legs was bent in a strange way. Oh, this was terrible!

"What happened to you?" I said.

One of his eyes was swollen shut. He looked battered, like one of those boxer guys on TV after a fight. I had to do something. I'd take him inside and wash off the blood and see how bad the cuts were.

I bent down to pick him up.

"Rourrr!" A front paw darted out and scratched me.

"Oh!" Now I was bleeding too, down my arm. "What'd you do that for? I'm trying to help you."

Didn't he trust me? Maybe he was just scared. And he'd come to the trailer. That must mean something. What should I do now?

Mrs. Holcomb. I ran to her door and knocked. Muffin started her silly yapping, but no one answered.

"Mrs. Holcomb!" I shouted. "It's me, Weezie!"

Finally the door opened.

"I'm sorry," said Mrs. Holcomb. "I was sewing on my machine. What's wrong?"

"It's Marmalade. He's hurt!"

"Marmalade?"

"That cat that hangs around here. That's what I call him. Come quick!"

She followed me to where he lay next to the step. His eyes were closed now. Oh no. Could he be dead?

Then his side moved a little, so I guessed he was still breathing.

"We've got to get him to a vet," she said.

I'd never seen Mrs. Holcomb move so fast. She ran inside and came back with a raggedy old towel and her garden gloves.

"In case he scratches," she told me. "I'll lift him and you put the towel under him. Ready?"

She did it so quick, Marmalade didn't have a chance to do anything. She carried him to her car and laid him down on the front seat.

"We'll take him to Doctor Fine," she said. "That's Muffy's vet. He's wonderful. If anyone can fix him up, he can."

I was surprised how fast she drove. Not like a little old lady at all. It was a good thing, because now Marmalade was acting funny. He was breathing really fast and struggling to get up.

"Wrap him in the towel," said Mrs. Holcomb. "Keep him warm."

I managed to get the towel around him, talking all the time.

"Hey, calm down. We're taking you to the doctor and he'll fix you up, no problem. Just lie still. That's all you have to do."

I patted him through the towel.

"Remember how I gave you all that tuna? You know I wouldn't hurt you. And it's okay that you scratched me. I know you were scared."

I felt him starting to quiet down, but he was still shaking.

"Good boy, Marmalade. Don't worry. I'm going to take good care of you. You can trust me."

It really seemed like he did. His good eye closed again and he stopped shaking. I looked down at him. Only the top of his head peeked out of the towel. Should I? This was my chance.

I reached down one finger and stroked his head. His fur was so soft. And he didn't move. Not one little bit.

I'd touched him. Finally. Like I'd wanted to for so long. Like the man with the bear cub. And he hadn't moved or scratched. Despite everything, I couldn't help smiling.

Then we were at the vet's office. I carried Marmalade inside.

"This is an emergency," Mrs. Holcomb told the woman at the desk, firm as could be, and we walked right past a girl with a big spotted dog into Doctor Fine's office.

He was young, with black hair only at the sides of his head. The top was shiny bald.

"Mrs. Holcomb," he said. "What's up?" Then he saw all the blood. "Lay him down on the table."

He examined Marmalade all over, talking softly to him and to us at the same time.

"Lie still for me, boy. That's right. What's his name?"

"Marmalade."

"Nice name. Cuts aren't too deep, except the one on his tail. Got to watch that for infection. Leg's hurt, but not broken. Not sure about the ribs."

Finally, he straightened up and looked at us.

"It appears he's been in a fight with something bigger than he is. Dog or raccoon maybe. But he could have been hit by a car. I'm going to have to keep him for a couple of days to check him out."

"Will he be alright?" I asked. He had to be.

Doctor Fine hesitated. "I can't be sure. But he's a tough old bird. So yes, I think your cat will be alright."

My cat.

"He's not—" I started to say. But then I stopped.

Marmalade came to me when he was hurt. He came to me.

"Thanks, Doctor Fine," I said.

Too Wild

Dr. Fine kept Marmalade for two days and then sent him home. We were supposed to keep him quiet for a few more days.

"He can stay at my place," said Mrs. Holcomb. She'd paid the vet bill, which was really nice of her. "I know your momma doesn't care for cats. But you can come and visit him."

She brought Marmalade home in the morning while I was at school. I couldn't wait to see him. The minute I got off the school bus, I started running up the hill.

Would his cuts be healed up? Was his tail okay? What if Marmalade really liked it at Mrs. Holcomb's house? She had all those doggy treats, which maybe cats liked too. He might want to stay and then I could see him all the time.

I was out of breath and had a stitch in my side when I knocked on Mrs. Holcomb's door.

"Mrs. Holcomb!" I called.

It was quiet inside. Muffin wasn't even barking.

"It's me, Weezie!"

Mrs. Holcomb came to the door. "Come in, Weezie."

I went inside. But where was Marmalade? I thought he'd be right there waiting for me. And where was Muffin?

"Where is he?" I asked. "Is he okay?"

She gave me a strange look. "I'm sure he is," she said. "But he isn't here."

How could that be? She said she'd keep him at her house.

"I'm sorry, Weezie," she said. "I tried, I really did. But he wouldn't calm down. He was all over the place, climbing the curtains, scratching at the door, trying to get out. He scared Muffin so, she hid under the bed and still won't come out. I had to let him go."

"Go?"

"Yes. I let him out. I'm sorry."

She did look sorry. But how could she do that?

"What about Doctor Fine?" I said. "He said to keep him quiet a few days."

"That's just it. He was acting so crazy, I was afraid he'd hurt himself. Doctor Fine said he was almost recovered. And he knows how to take care of himself. He'll be alright."

"But—" I started again. I couldn't say it. *I wanted him to stay. I wanted him to be my cat.*

Mrs. Holcomb looked at me with her kind eyes.

"He can't be shut up inside. He's just too wild. If you'd seen him, you'd understand. I know you care about him, Weezie. But don't worry, he'll come back."

"He will?" I wasn't so sure.

She reached out and squeezed my shoulder.

"He will, honey. He will."

Smoke

Calvin was glad to ride me to the library on Saturday.

"Are we doing another investion?" he asked.

"Yes," I said. "Only this one is different."

"Why?"

I tapped my finger on my forehead. "Because we're just using our brains this time."

Calvin grinned. "I like using my brain," he said.

Louella was waiting inside the door.

"Hi, Calvin," she said.

"Hi." He looked up at the ceiling. "Wow, it's big! I never went to the libary before."

"It's full of books," I said. "You can look at them if you want."

"Okay!"

"So, Weezie," said Louella. "I was thinking the library might not want kids looking at those old newspapers. Because we might rip them or something."

I hadn't thought of that.

"But my momma knows the librarian, Mrs. Henderson, from church. If I ask her nicely, maybe she'll let us."

Sure enough, Mrs. Henderson was glad to help.

"It's for school, isn't it?"

Louella nodded.

"Well, I'm sure you'll be careful."

Louella had told a lie! Even though she hadn't said anything. I guess there are all kinds of lies, even ones you don't say out loud.

"We keep the newspapers downstairs," said Mrs. Henderson. "I'll show you."

Calvin was staring at a book on a nearby table. *The Great Big Book of Trucks* was the title.

"Could I read that book?" he asked.

"Sure," I said. And then, "See ya later, Potater!"

He grinned.

We left Calvin with the truck book and followed

Mrs. Henderson to a small room downstairs. It was crammed with file cabinets.

"No one comes here much," she said, "so it's a little dusty."

She showed us the one with the old newspapers.

"I hope you find what you're looking for," she said. "Just let me know if you need help."

"Thanks, Mrs. Henderson," said Louella.

I opened the top drawer. Inside were rows of folders, each neatly labeled with the month and year.

"What year should we start with?" asked Louella.

I'd kind of figured it out. Momma must have met my daddy when she was fifteen or sixteen. That would make it 1975 or 1976. And some time in the fall, in football season.

So we kept going backwards till we got to the fall of 1976. We piled the folders on a small table.

"I'll look at August and September," I said. "And you take October and November."

As soon as I opened the first one, I started sneezing.

"Mrs. Henderson was right about the dust," I said. "I bet no one's looked at these for years."

The Star Ledger was excited about the football team in August. "Coach Predicts Winning Season," said a headline. And then "Yellowjackets Sting Bixby in First Game."

"Bixby," I said. "Maybe my daddy was from there."

Louella wrote it down in her little notebook.

In September, it was "Yellowjackets Streak by Broken Arrow." And "Muskogee Shoots Down Yellowjackets in Close Contest." And "Yellowjackets Nip Bartlesville, 37-35."

It looked like the coach was right. The team was having a good season.

Louella wrote down each town my daddy might be from.

"Hey," she said suddenly. "Look at this!"

There it was. The newspaper picture of Momma and Marcella with the bee! And underneath, the caption we hadn't been able to read: "Pep Squad members Charlene Dawson and Marcella Stuckley with Yellowjacket mascot Billy Perkins at Friday's Homecoming game."

"So that's it," said Louella. "Your momma was on the Pep Squad."

"And the bee was a boy," I said. Probably he cheered too, and ran around pretending to sting people.

But it hadn't worked at the Homecoming game.

"Sapulpa Smokes the Yellowjackets," read the headline.

I stared at it.

Smokes, it said. *Smoke.*

Could that mean something? Probably not.

I looked at the first line of the story.

"Sapulpa quarterback Wade 'Smoke' Nealy ran rings around the Yellowjackets Friday night, ruining Homecoming for hometown fans."

It was like I was dreaming. I couldn't believe it.

"Louella," I said pointing. "Read this."

"Oh," she said. Then, "Wow! That's him. Your daddy!"

It had to be. I stared at the paper. Yes, the name was really there. Wade "Smoke" Nealy.

We read the rest of the story together. Sapulpa's star quarterback was nicknamed "Smoke" because he could escape being tackled, like he was made of smoke. He'd run for three touchdowns and passed for two more to beat the Yellowjackets. "With Nealy as quarterback," the story ended, "it looks like Sapulpa could be headed for the state championships."

"Wade Nealy," I said out loud. Finally I knew his name. And the town he was from. Sapulpa.

Louella was super excited. "You know what that means? We can find him now! All we have to do is look in the Sapulpa phonebook."

That was true. All of a sudden, it was easy.

"I bet Mrs. Henderson has one," said Louella.

We put everything back in the file cabinet and ran upstairs.

"Did you find what you needed?" asked Mrs. Henderson.

"Yes, thank you," said Louella. "Do you have a Sapulpa phonebook we could borrow?"

"Of course."

My fingers were shaking as I hunted through the phonebook for the N's. Na, Nap, Nat, Ne, Nea. And finally, I found it. Nealy, Curtis. Nealy, Flora. Nealy, Wallace.

But no Nealy, Wade.

I came down to earth with a thud. "He's not there," I said.

"Are you sure?" Louella peered over my shoulder.

"I'm sure."

"I guess he must have moved."

Of course. He was grown up now. He could have moved anywhere.

"But those other Nealys," Louella said. "Most likely they're relatives of his. Hey!" Suddenly she was excited again. "I bet if you call them, you can find out where he is now."

That made sense. I'd do it.

Louella wrote the names and phone numbers in

her notebook, ripped out the page, and handed it to me.

"We're getting close," she said. "Really close. You're going to find him, Weezie."

Yes, I was, I thought as I rode home, holding tight to Calvin's shirt with one hand and *The Great Big Book of Trucks* with the other. *I really was.*

Three Nealys

It was funny the way things turned out. My daddy's relatives lived just a few miles away. They'd been there my whole life and I never knew it. I'd done all that investigating, riding all over the place on Calvin's bike, and they were right there all along. If only I'd known my daddy's last name and the town he came from, I could have found him pretty fast myself.

Which was why Momma never would tell me, I thought.

But I hadn't found him yet. I still had to make those phone calls.

"When are you going to call?" Louella asked. "This weekend?"

I nodded. I didn't feel quite so sure about it now.

How was I going to do it? What would I say? Where could I call from?

Not the trailer, that was for sure. I needed to be far away from Momma. Not Louella's house, where I wasn't allowed to go anyway A phone booth somewhere—that was the best plan. There was one outside the Star Drugstore downtown.

"Let me know as soon as you find out anything, okay?" said Louella. "You promise?"

"I promise."

I woke up Saturday morning feeling antsy inside. This could be the day. If only Momma would take Ruth Ann and Jackson someplace and leave me alone. Just about every Saturday she did, but with my luck, this time she wouldn't.

But right after breakfast she said, "I hear there's rides set up in the Walmart parking lot. I'm going to take Ruth Ann and Jackson over for a while. Want to come?"

It was the most she'd said to me since the day I ran off with Roy.

"No thanks," I said.

"You always liked that Tilt-a-Whirl. I bet they'll have that."

It almost seemed like she was trying to make up with me.

"My stomach's not feeling so good," I said. Which was true. All of a sudden it was kind of queasy.

"Well, you better stay home then. You can straighten up the place."

Yes, Momma. That's what I always said to her. But I wasn't going to say it anymore.

I didn't say anything.

The three of them drove off, and I was free. I almost wished I wasn't, I was feeling so strange. Excited and scared at the same time. This might be the day I finally found my daddy. But oh, I wished Gramma Emmeline was here to hold my hand.

That made me think of those bits of her teapot I'd saved in Jackson's sock. I took out the sock and put it in my pocket, just for luck.

You can do this, I thought. *You have to. It will be good.*

I went to find Calvin. He was sitting next to a little racetrack he'd built in the dirt, racing his cars around.

"It's the Indy 500," he told me. "Carson James is in the lead. Bart Connelly just crashed."

"Hey, Calvin," I said. "Want to ride me to town?"

"Are we doing another invection?"

"Yes, we are."

"At the libary?"

"No, but you'll get to look at car magazines."

His round face broke into a wide grin. "Okay, let's go!"

This time the ride to town seemed over in a minute. And there I was in front of the Star Drugstore.

"I have to make a couple of calls," I told Calvin. "You go inside and look at car magazines. Or buy yourself a candy bar."

"Okay."

He went inside, and I went into the phone booth. My hands felt sweaty as I got out the quarters I'd taken from Momma's coin jar. It wasn't stealing. I just wouldn't have lunch Monday.

Just as I was about to drop in the money, my hand froze. What if my daddy was as bad as Momma said? Did I really want to meet him? He'd never wanted to meet me, his own baby, not once in all these years.

But if I didn't do this now, I'd always wonder. And I'd always have his name stuck in my head.

I took a deep breath and called the first number. Curtis Nealy.

"Hello!" a man's deep voice boomed out.

"Uh—hello," I said. "I'm—um—looking for a man named Wade Nealy. Can you tell me where he is?"

"Whadja say? Speak up!"

He sounded old, and deaf too.

"Wade Nealy," I said louder. "I'm looking for him. Is he a relative of yours?"

"Ray? You're looking for Ray?"

"No, Wade!" I was practically shouting.

"Don't know nothin' 'bout no Wade. No one like that in this family."

And *click*, he hung up.

That was no help. What if none of these Nealys knew anything about my daddy? I'd be back where I started.

I dialed the next name. Flora Nealy.

"Hello. Nealy residence."

The voice sounded young. At least she'd be able to hear me.

"Is this Flora Nealy?"

"No, she's away right now. Can I help you with something?"

She sounded nice.

"I'm looking for Wade Nealy. Do you know, is he a relative of hers?"

"I don't know anything about that," the voice answered. "I'm just taking care of her cat. But she'll be back in a week. You can call her then."

A whole week. That seemed so long.

"Um, do you think I could call her where she is? It's really important."

"Well, if it's important, I guess you could." She didn't sound too sure. "She's in Oklahoma City visiting her sister."

She told me the number, only I didn't have a pencil to write it down, so I had to keep saying it over and over inside my head. And Oklahoma City was pretty far away. How much would it cost to call there?

I ran inside. Calvin was sitting on the floor looking at racecar magazines.

"Do you have any quarters?" Usually he did because his gramma gave him all her change.

He pulled out a few coins. "But I was going to buy a candy bar like you said."

"I'll pay you back. I'll buy you two candy bars!"

Now I wouldn't be having lunch on Tuesday either.

I ran back to the phone booth. Was that number 7335 or 7533? 7335, I was pretty sure. I punched in the number.

"Hello?"

This time the voice sounded older.

"Is Flora Nealy there?" I asked.

"Just a minute."

After a long minute, I heard a soft, husky voice say, "Hello."

"You don't know me," I said real fast. "But I'm trying to find Wade Nealy. Could you tell me if you might be related to him?"

The voice didn't answer right away. And then it said, "Why do you want to know? Who is this?"

My heart thumped loud in my ears. It seemed like she knew the name. This could be the right Nealy.

"My name is Grace Louise Dawson," I said and stopped. What should I say now? Well, I might as well come out with it.

"I want to know because—because Wade Nealy is my daddy."

I heard her take in a long breath. Then nothing. Maybe she'd fainted or something.

Finally her voice came back, kind of gruff.

"Wade Nealy is my son's name. But he doesn't have any children. He never was married."

"Uh—" This was hard to say. "It was when he was in high school that I was born. He and my momma weren't married. Her name is Charlene Dawson."

There was a long silence. Then, "Oh. I see."

That was all, but I could tell she knew the name.

"Well," she said after a minute, "this is news to

me. You say your name is Grace Louise? And how old are you?"

"Almost eleven," I said.

Another silence. She sure didn't seem overjoyed. Maybe she didn't believe me. But why would I make up a story like that?

"I think we should meet," she said finally. "I'll be home next week. And I'd like to talk to your momma too."

"Okay."

But Flora Nealy hadn't said anything about what I really wanted to know.

"That would be nice," I said. "Getting to meet you, I mean. But I really want to find my daddy."

"Yes, I know."

"Where is he at now? Could you please tell me?"

She didn't say anything for the longest time. And then, "I'm sorry to have to tell you this, but your daddy is dead."

Dead? The word banged around in my head. How could it be? Of all the things I'd imagined about him, I'd never figured on that. He wasn't old like Gramma Emmeline. Why, he couldn't be more than thirty years old. That was way too young to die.

I couldn't think of what to say. And Flora Nealy was silent on the other end.

Finally she said, "He died in a fishing boat accident." Her voice sounded far away, farther than Oklahoma City. "Up in Alaska."

Alaska? How did he get there?

"It's a long story. I'll tell you about it when we meet. Goodbye, Grace Louise."

"Goodbye," I said. And the phone clicked off.

I stood there, still holding it. My hand was shaking.

After all this time, I'd finally found my daddy. And now it turned out he was dead. How could that be?

Standing Tall

I t had been two days and I still couldn't believe it.
Could my daddy really be dead? Drowned in
the ocean way up in Alaska? Or was this some kind
of weird dream? Maybe I hadn't gotten the right
Nealy on the phone after all.

But I had. I knew I had.

It seemed so strange, though. How could the boy
in that photograph get from playing football in a
little Oklahoma town to working on a fishing boat
in Alaska?

I tried to picture him on a fishing boat. What kind
of boat was it? And what kind of fish did they have
in Alaska anyway? All I could see in my mind were

those pretty blue and gold ones on a coral reef I saw one time on a nature show. But that was someplace warm, like Florida. Alaska wasn't warm. The ocean there must be freezing cold.

Then a new picture popped into my mind. Of a giant wave sweeping that boy off the boat into icy water.

Suddenly I was shivering like I was the one dropped in the ocean. I looked over to see if Momma had noticed. But she was folding laundry, her eyes glued to her game show on TV. She always thought she could do better than the real contestants and win a trip to Mexico or something.

I had to stop thinking about my daddy and study for tomorrow's math test. Opening the book, I stared at the practice problems. Why did all those numbers just look like squiggles to me?

The phone rang.

"That'll be Frankie," Momma grumbled. "Wanting to change my shift again."

But it wasn't Frankie, I could tell. Or Roy either. Because Momma was talking in her polite voice. Maybe it was Mrs. Hitchins.

She hung up the phone and walked over and shut off the TV. She turned, staring straight at me.

"What did you do?" she demanded.

"Me?"

"Yes, you. That was someone claiming to be your daddy's momma. Says you called her. Says she wants to meet both of us."

Oh lordy me. Flora Nealy! I thought she'd wait till she got home to call. I was going to tell Momma about her. I just needed time to get used to my daddy being dead.

"Well? You did call her, didn't you?"

I couldn't lie. And I couldn't speak. I just nodded.

"So. Let me get this straight. I told you a hundred times that you don't want to know about your miserable excuse for a daddy. But you go behind my back and find out about him somehow and call up his momma. And now she wants to come and meet us." Her voice grew louder. "What about him, Weezie? Is he coming too?"

She didn't know. Momma really didn't know.

"He can't!" I cried. "My daddy's dead!"

That took her back.

"He died in a fishing boat accident. Up in Alaska."

For a minute she looked stunned. Her mouth pinched up, like maybe she was a little bit sorry. Only for a minute, though.

"I'm not going to ask you about that," she said. "Or how you found him. The thing is, you did what

I told you not to do. How do you think that makes me feel?"

"Bad," I mumbled.

"You bet it does! Here I've been taking care of you all these years, protecting you from him, making sure you don't grow up like him, and what do you do? You go against your own mother!" She was so angry, she was shaking. She raised her hand. I thought for a minute she was going to slap me.

Go ahead, I thought. *That will just prove you hate me.*

Momma's hand hung in the air. Then she smacked it against her forehead and sank down in her chair.

It was so quiet, I could hear my own breathing. And a little cry from the bedroom. Ruth Ann. Momma's yelling had woken her up. That was good. She could save me. But then it stopped. Probably she was just having a dream.

Momma sat slouched in her chair. She looked like she was somewhere else, somewhere far away.

"That woman hated me," she said. "Only met me a few times, but I could tell. Wouldn't give me the time of day, like I wasn't good enough for her precious son."

She straightened up and her face got hard.

"Here's what we're going to do. You're going to call her back and tell her you changed your mind.

You don't want to meet her and you don't want to know anything else about your no-good daddy."

I couldn't do that. What did Gramma Emmeline used to say? What's done can't be undone.

No, I wouldn't do it. This was my time to speak up, like Roy said.

I opened my mouth, but nothing came out.

"You call her now," said Momma, "and this will be over."

She stared at me, waiting for me to say, "Yes, Momma," like I always did.

"No," I said, so soft I barely heard it myself.

"What did you say?"

I swallowed hard. "No. I won't call her."

Momma looked at me like I'd gone crazy.

"You understand, this is the woman who raised up your daddy. I bet she told him to run out on me. Likely gave him the money to do it too. I'm not having anything to do with her. And you're not either. I won't allow it."

I could see myself stuck in my trailer prison all summer. But I didn't care. All of a sudden, I felt calm.

"I need to meet my daddy's momma," I said. "Even if she's bad like you say. I need to do it."

Why couldn't Momma understand that? She just kept looking at me, shaking her head.

"I'll do it some way. I will, Momma."

Still no answer. I could be hard like her. I felt it happening inside me. I looked straight into her eyes that were boring into mine.

"You can't stop me. I'll go behind your back like you said. I bet Roy would take me on his bike."

She kept staring at me for a long minute. Then her eyes went to the floor. She seemed to shrink, like all the air had gone out of her.

I'd won. I felt light all over. *I did it, Roy!* I thought. I'd stood up to Momma.

Only looking at her sitting there, still not understanding, it didn't feel quite as good as I'd thought it would.

Pancake Heaven

Flora means flower, Louella told me. She should know, seeing as her momma is so big on flowers.

Flora Nealy didn't look like a flower. More like one of those skinny weeds that grow by the side of the road. She had wispy, goldy-gray hair and her face was wrinkled, as if she'd been out in the sun a lot.

So this was my new gramma. She wasn't like Gramma Emmeline, with her big, warm lap that I'd been missing for so long. This gramma's lap wouldn't be like hers. I squeezed the sock with the teapot pieces that I'd stuffed in my pocket again for luck.

We sat across from each other at Pancake Heaven. That was the only place Momma would let me meet her. But Momma wasn't going to have anything to do with that woman, she'd told me again this morning.

"You look a lot like him."

That was the first thing Flora Nealy said to me. She sat there, just staring and staring. It made me feel funny.

"I know," I said. Momma had told me that enough times.

She just kept staring. She wasn't smiling, like it was a good thing I looked like her son. Grammas were supposed to smile. Gramma Emmeline did all the time.

Out of the corner of my eye, I saw Momma watching us. She hadn't said one word to Flora Nealy, not even hello. Just plunked down a cup of coffee in front of her and walked away.

"So it's true," said Flora Nealy. "You really are Wade's child."

I guessed she hadn't totally believed me on the phone. She had to see for herself. She still didn't seem real happy about it, though.

"Now I know why he ran off to California the way he did. It never really made sense to me."

California? I thought it was Alaska. I was all mixed up. And mixed up about her. Was she just here to see if I looked like her son, not because she cared about me? Was that why she didn't seem friendly?

Flora Nealy took a sip of her coffee. After a minute she said, "Well, never mind. I suppose we should get to know each other, Grace Louise. Tell me a little about yourself."

So I did. I told her about my little sister and brother and how we lived at Happy Days Trailer Park and I was in the fifth grade at school. Then she told me some things about her life. How she grew up in the country but moved to Sapulpa when her husband got a job with the railroad. He died three years ago. She had two daughters and three grandkids. And a cat named Rosalie.

I'd forgotten about the cat. "What kind is it?" I asked.

"An old gray tabby. She sleeps in the front window. Wouldn't even move if a mouse ran by."

Not like Marmalade, who wasn't mine at all.

She still hadn't said one word about my daddy. But I had to know.

I reached for the syrup pitcher, twirling it around. It was sticky, like Momma always said. I took a deep breath and said, "Would you please tell me about my daddy?"

Flora Nealy looked down at her coffee cup. For a minute, I thought she wasn't going to answer. Then she said, "Wade was my baby. Came along a few years after the girls. Just the sweetest little boy you'd ever want to meet."

For the first time, she almost smiled.

"From the time he was little, he loved trucks. If we were out in the car, he'd be pointing them out, telling you the make and model. His daddy was so proud. He liked to show him off to his friends."

She looked proud herself, remembering.

"Then, when Wade got older, it was football. I don't know which he loved more. When he was in high school, he pumped gas till he saved enough to buy a second-hand truck. From then on, he was either at football practice or working on that truck of his."

I remembered how happy he looked standing by that truck.

"It was at a football game he must have met your momma. I met her a few times, and I remember him driving over to see her. But I didn't think much about it. Lots of girls liked Wade."

I glanced over at Momma, but she wasn't looking at us, just filling sugar bowls next to frowning Frankie.

"One morning Wade just up and said he was leaving. He was going to drive out to California and stay with his sister Glenda while he looked for a job. Randall—that was my husband—was so mad. He called him a fool and every other name for not finishing high school when he was so close. But Wade wouldn't listen. He loaded up his truck and left a couple of days later."

She stopped, looking straight at me.

"He never told me his real reason for leaving, that he was about to become a daddy. Never mentioned your momma at all."

She picked up her coffee cup and set it down. It must be cold by now. I could see she'd like to stop talking, but she had to finish the story.

"He was out there a couple of years, just working at fast-food places and jobs like that. Then he heard you could make good money in Alaska, working on a fishing boat. So he and a friend went up there. We got a few phone calls, saying it was hard work but the pay was good. He sounded happy. Then one night his friend called, saying there'd been an accident. A storm came up real sudden and they were caught in it, and Wade was swept overboard. Drowned in the ocean."

All of a sudden Flora Nealy's eyes filled up with tears.

"I never did see the ocean, and my son drowned in it. Isn't that something? He was only twenty-two years old."

So. Finally I knew.

I couldn't think what to say. I slid the syrup pitcher from one hand to the other. Now they were both sticky. I tried to wipe them with a napkin, but that sticky stuff wouldn't come off.

"I understand this is a lot to take in," Flora Nealy said, "when you never knew anything about him."

It was. Alaska of all places. Who'd have guessed he'd end up there? In the freezing cold water of Alaska, not with me in Florida like I'd imagined. I'd found out a little about my daddy's life. Only I still didn't know him. And now I never would because he was dead.

"I know your momma must hate Wade for what he did," she said. "It wasn't right. But he was young and scared. Too scared to do the right thing. He wasn't a bad boy really."

She would say that. She was his momma. The thing was, he never came back. He knew he had a little baby in Oklahoma. He could have come back instead of going way up to Alaska and getting himself killed. He could have if he cared.

I didn't know what to think. Was he bad or not?

"Don't hate him," Flora Nealy said. "Please."

I looked up at her. Tears were leaking out now, rolling down her wrinkly cheeks.

"A child should never die before his momma," she said. "It isn't right. That boy was the light of my life. And now he's gone."

A Regular Cat

Marmalade came back the next day. One minute he wasn't there and the next he was, sitting on Mrs. Holcomb's step same as always.

I blinked. After the way he'd torn up her house, I wasn't sure I'd ever see him again. But here he was, and looking good, like he was all healed up.

"Hi," I said.

Marmalade looked at me with those eyes that seemed as if they could see right inside a person.

I wished I could see inside him. Had he come back to show me he was okay? Or maybe to thank me for rescuing him? Or was it just for the food?

It didn't really matter. He was here now. I could talk to him like before.

"I found out about my daddy," I told him. "He died way up in Alaska. I thought I could find him, but I couldn't. Well, I did, but he was dead."

It still felt weird to me, him dying so far away. And so young. Only twenty-two. I was about half his age already. But maybe if I kept saying it out loud, it would start to seem real.

"My daddy is dead," I said again. "And I never knew him. I wish I could have met him one time. Just to see what he was like."

Marmalade was settled down now, his eyes half-closed. But his ears pricked up as if he was listening.

"I met his momma, my gramma. But she's not like my old gramma at all. She seemed real sad, and I don't know if she likes me. She has a cat, but it's not like you. Hers likes to sleep all day and wouldn't even care if a mouse came walking by. You'd care. You'd have it for lunch, I bet."

Marmalade's pink tongue flicked out. Did he know what I was talking about? It always seemed like he did.

"Everything's mixed up," I said. "My daddy being

dead and now this new gramma, and Momma. Specially Momma. She hates me, you know."

That was the worst part—Momma hating me. Just thinking about it made me feel empty inside.

"Can you believe it?" I said. "Her own little girl."

If Marmalade was a regular cat, he'd jump down from his step now and come over to me. He'd curl up next to me and purr and I could stroke that soft spot on top of his head.

But he wasn't a regular cat. He never would be. Like Mrs. Holcomb said, he was too wild. And not about to let himself be tamed or owned by anyone.

That was okay, I thought. We could still be friends. I liked how tough he was, how he took care of himself and didn't need anyone. Except when he was hurt. He'd come to me then, and I was pretty sure he would again. This hadn't turned out the way I'd hoped, like the man with the bear cub. But maybe close enough.

Marmalade arched his back and stretched, first his front legs, then the back ones. It looked like he was leaving.

"Hey," I said. "Thanks for letting me pat you that one time. I'll put out more food and you'll come back, right? Maybe I can get Momma to buy fish sticks. You'd like them, I bet."

Marmalade's tail did that little swish thing, like he agreed. He jumped down. Off to do some hunting in the tall grass, it looked like.

"Take care of yourself," I said. "And don't get into any more fights."

He gave me a look that said, *Maybe I will and maybe I won't.* And then—I couldn't believe it—as he passed by, I felt him brush against my leg. So light and soft, it was barely a touch. But it was.

Then he was gone, into the tall grass.

Pieces of Gramma

Shool was almost over. Today was our last art
class before everything had to be cleaned up
and put away.

"What's this?" I said when I walked in the door.

It looked like a big mess. All kinds of stuff was
laid out on the tables. The usual paper, paint, glue,
markers, and clay. But also stacks of soda-pop cans,
cardboard tubes, newspapers, and magazines. And
piles of little things: paper clips, pipe cleaners, ribbon, buttons, beads, popsicle sticks, gum wrappers,
even little plastic animals.

"Today is Let Your Imagination Run Wild Day,"
Ms. Martinelli announced. "You can make anything

you like. Experiment with all the materials. But most of all, have fun!"

For a minute, everyone just stared. Then Farley Wilcox began scooping up cardboard tubes. "I'm going to make a snake!" he said.

"I'm making a fighter plane!" said Bobby Flack, going for the popsicle sticks.

"What are you going to do?" I asked Louella.

"I want to use everything! I think I'll make a collage."

She started cutting pictures out of magazines.

What did I want to make? I wandered over to the clay table, and picked up a chunk of the gray stuff. It felt good in my hands, cool and damp and nicely squishy. I rolled it between my hands so it grew longer. It could be a snake, like Farley's. But I didn't want to make a snake. I patted it into a ball.

I poked a hole in my clay ball, then another. Those could be eyes. Below them, I pinched the clay to make a nose, kind of fat. And below that, I scooped out a mouth. I turned it up into a smile, and just like that, I had a face.

I half-closed my eyes to see what popped out at me. And what popped out was Gramma Emmeline. That made me smile. Oh, if I could make this look like her, it would be the best thing! Ever since I'd met that new gramma, Flora Nealy, I'd been missing my old one more than ever.

Gramma Emmeline had round cheeks, I remembered. I piled up the clay on both sides of the nose and smoothed it out. I couldn't remember her ears, so I just made them small. Now for the hair. That was the hardest part. Hers was always frizzed up.

"Like I stuck my hand in a light socket," Gramma Emmeline used to say.

I tried pinching the clay at the top of her head into tufts, but that looked weird. Then I twisted little bits of it into curls and stuck them on. Better, but still not right.

"That's coming along nicely, Weezie." Ms. Martinelli leaned over me, her bracelets clinking in my ear. "Are you going to make the rest of her?"

I hadn't thought of that. Why not? A whole Gramma Emmeline would be even better than just her head.

"Yes," I said.

All of a sudden I remembered something Gramma used to do. She'd be waiting to take her biscuits out of the oven, the radio playing her favorite country music. And she'd just start dancing. Twirling around the kitchen table, bouncing and laughing.

"I can't help it," she'd say. "That Johnny Cash gives me dancing feet!"

That's what I wanted to make: Gramma Emmeline dancing.

So I squeezed more clay into a body, round in the middle like Gramma was. I stuck on arms, hands on her hips. Then legs. Those took awhile to get right, one bent like she was kicking, one straight. And last I made that apron she always wore, flying out the way it did when she danced.

I sat back and looked. It was almost her, only the eyes weren't bright blue like Gramma's. And the hair wasn't right at all.

I got up and walked around, looking at what other kids were doing. Farley's snake took up a whole table. He was painting it green. Two other boys were building a weird–looking animal out of cans. Louella's head was bent over her collage.

"Let me see," I said.

She'd glued pictures of flowers all over a piece of cardboard. Now she was adding more, made out of bits of ribbon, buttons, and beads.

"That looks great," I said. It really did.

"I love collages," she said, "because you don't have to draw anything. Maybe I'll give it to my daddy."

That gave me an idea. I picked up two bright blue beads and some pipe cleaners and markers, and went back to the clay table. I pushed the beads into the eyeholes I'd made. Perfect! Then I colored a bunch of pipe cleaners orange, twisted them into curls, and stuck them on top of Gramma's head.

She really looked as if she'd stuck her hand in a light socket. I liked it!

Gramma Emmeline would too if she could see it.

One thing still wasn't right. Gramma's apron was so gray. Not a bit like the flowered one she used to wear. Maybe I could cut out flowers like Louella had and stick them on.

And then I had the best idea yet.

"Can I get something from my book bag?" I asked Ms. Martinelli.

"Sure," she said.

I ran to my classroom, and ran back. Untying Jackson's sock, I poured out the bits of Gramma Emmeline's teapot. They glittered, pink and white with flashes of gold, on the dark table. Just right for Gramma's apron.

I stuck the pieces every which way into the clay. And little by little, the apron changed from dull gray to pink, dotted with roses.

Now, finally, Gramma Emmeline looked just

right. I could almost see her dancing around the kitchen table while I sat eating a warm biscuit with honcy just out of the oven.

"She sure looks happy!" said Ms. Martinelli behind me. "Is it someone special?"

"My gramma," I said. "She died a long time ago."

"Oh, I'm sorry." I felt her hand on my shoulder. "But you've made something wonderful to remember her by."

Yes, I had.

I could never forget her now. Gramma Emmeline would always be with me.

No More Lies

"That's one crazy gramma!" said Farley.

"I love her apron," said Louella. "Did she really used to dance when she took care of you?"

"Whenever Johnny Cash came on the radio," I said. "She said he gave her dancing feet."

We were packing everything up to take home on the last day of school.

"You take good care of her now," Ms. Martinelli told me. "She's really special."

I nodded. "I will."

"And Weezie," she went on, "I hope you'll be coming to my art class this summer. We'll be sketching outdoors and going on field trips. I'm planning a visit to a craft museum and to my art studio and a couple of others. There's still time to sign up."

Oh, that would be so good! But I had to look after Ruth Ann and Jackson every day while Momma was at work.

"I don't know," I said. "I'll try."

"Well, if you can't join us, be sure to do some drawing on your own, okay? You've got talent."

Ms. Martinelli seemed really serious. Her gold hoop earrings gleamed in the sun.

"Okay."

She smiled. "Have a good summer, Weezie."

Louella was waiting for me in the hall.

"Did she tell you about her art class? And going to her studio? We'll get to see her sculptures! Can you believe she made one out of nothing but bowling balls? You have to sign up!"

Yes! I thought.

I really, really wanted to go to that art class. Momma would say it was a waste of time since drawing would never pay the rent, but I'd make her change her mind. I'd stood up to her about seeing Flora Nealy, and I could do it again. I knew I could.

Roy was doing it too. He called all the time now, telling Momma he wanted to see Jackson. It seemed like she was starting to give in a little.

The last time he called, I answered and he said he was sorry he'd gotten us arrested, but I should remember what he told me.

"Hang in there, Weezie," he said.

"I will," I told him.

I planned to do that, too.

Louella and I walked to the front door, where the buses were just pulling in. Mine was in front.

"See you tomorrow," I said. "Oops, not really!"

Louella laughed. "Well, soon anyway. At the art class, right?"

"Right." Somehow I was going to make it happen.

I sat in my usual seat next to Calvin, holding my clay Gramma carefully in my lap.

What would Momma say when she saw it? Maybe she'd frown the way she always did about my art. Maybe she'd be mad that I'd used Gramma's broken teapot pieces for the apron. Or maybe—could it happen?—she might like it.

And maybe, I realized suddenly, I didn't care if she liked it or not. Because I did like it.

Calvin did too

"She's so sparkly," he said.

Sparkly. That was the right word for Gramma Emmeline. She was always sparkly.

"You're a good artist," said Calvin. "Could you make me a picture of a racecar sometime?"

"Sure," I said.

Calvin beamed. It didn't take much to make him happy. After all he'd done for me, riding me all over on his bike, at least I could draw him a racecar picture.

I wanted to draw Marmalade some more too. Crouched in the grass, about to pounce on a mouse. Sitting looking at me the way he did. I wanted to draw his punched-in face with that tough-guy look that said *don't mess with me*.

Tough, that was Marmalade. He had a shell around him like the turtle Calvin and I found one time in the woods. Calvin poked it with a stick and it went inside its shell and wouldn't come out.

Momma was like that too, I thought. Hiding inside her shell, holding on to her hates. Most likely she'd always hate my daddy, even though he was dead. And his momma on account of him. And me too. No, that wasn't quite right. It wasn't that she hated me exactly. She just didn't love me. Couldn't even hug me after she thought I'd been kidnapped. That's what hurt so bad.

I squeezed my eyes shut. A wave of pain washed

over me, like it was flowing through my blood. Every part of me ached.

That minute I decided something. I wasn't going to hate my daddy. Maybe he was bad or maybe just young, going off and leaving me. It didn't matter. He was dead now anyway. I didn't want to be like Momma, filled up with hating.

"Hey, Weezie," said a voice behind me.

Ruby. I thought she was sitting in back. She must have moved up.

"How's your daddy doing?" she asked in her fake-nice voice, sticking her head between Calvin and me.

I didn't answer.

She was practically breathing down my neck.

"Is he going to be home for the Fourth of July? You could take him to our picnic at Calvary Baptist and the fireworks down by the river."

I took a deep breath, then turned around and looked straight into her beady little eyes.

"My daddy is dead," I said. "He died in a fishing boat accident up in Alaska."

That surprised her.

"B-but," she stammered, "you said he was a truck driver."

"He never was," I said. "I just made that up. But I'm telling the truth now."

It felt good to finally be telling the truth. Clean, like after a bath. Telling those lies always made me feel squirmy inside, as if bugs were running around in my stomach.

"Oh. Well. That's too bad. I mean, about him being dead and all."

Ruby got up fast and went back to her seat.

Yes, it was too bad. And too bad about Momma being the way she was. But that's how the cookie crumbles, as Gramma Emmeline used to say. I couldn't do anything about it.

I had other people, though. Like Louella. And her momma and daddy. And Calvin. And Ms. Martinelli and Mrs. Holcomb. And Gramma Emmeline. She was still here, even if she wasn't really. I touched one of her pipe-cleaner curls and saw her smiling up at me.

Calvin nudged me with his elbow.

"Your daddy's really dead?"

"Yes."

"Then we're not going to do any more investing?"

"No. Not about him anyway."

"Oh."

He looked all sad, chewing on his lip.

"But we could do some other stuff this summer. Go places on your bike. Maybe build a real race-track out of wood and have races with your cars."

His face lit right up.

"And remember what I said. I'm going to draw you the biggest, best racecar picture you ever saw!"

"A red one? With Carson James driving it?"

"Absolutely."

The bus slowed down for our stop and Calvin and I got off.

"See ya later, Investigrater!" he said.

I had to smile. "Hey, Calvin, that was good!"

He gave me a goofy smile and ran off.

Holding my Gramma Emmeline tight, I walked slowly up the hill toward the trailer. And Momma.

Momma says I'm a bad girl. But I'm not.

I'm not.

JEAN VAN LEEUWEN is the author of more than fifty children's books, including picture books, Easy-to-Read books, and middle-grade fiction. She has won numerous awards, including the William Allen White Award, the South Carolina Children's Book Award, the Washington Irving Children's Choice Award as well as many ALA Notable Book citations. Her popular Oliver and Amanda Pig Easy-to-Read series was called as "timeless as the truths of childhood" by the *New York Times*. A former children's book editor, she lives in Chappaqua, New York.